"You've never forgiven yourself, have you?"

"I broke the rules," she said in a very low voice.

"And rules are important because they save a lot of trouble and grief. That goes for traffic rules, health rules, or sex. But having been in a wreck doesn't mean you have to agonize over it for the rest of your life."

"There's Grendel," Addy reminded him.

"She's a darling little girl."

Addy replied, "Yes," but she was distracted. Her whole body was responding to Sam's long fingers working lazy circles on her shoulders. Then he tugged her body back and turned her expertly so that she was pressed against him.

Her eyes pleaded with him. For what? Did she want to be taken or released? She didn't know. He took his time, touching her lingeringly, until she was nestled just right. And then he kissed her . . .

Dear Reader:

As the months go by, we continue to receive word from you that SECOND CHANCE AT LOVE romances are providing you with the kind of romantic entertainment you're looking for. In your letters you've voiced enthusiastic support for SECOND CHANCE AT LOVE, you've shared your thoughts on how personally meaningful the books are, and you've suggested ideas and changes for future books. Although we can't always reply to your letters as quickly as we'd like, please be assured that we appreciate your comments. Your thoughts are all-important to us!

We're glad many of you have come to associate SECOND CHANCE AT LOVE books with our butterfly trademark. We think the butterfly is a perfect symbol of the reaffirmation of life and thrilling new love that SECOND CHANCE AT LOVE heroines and heroes find together in each story. We hope you keep asking for the ''butterfly books,'' and that, when you buy one—whether by a favorite author or a talented new writer—you're sure of a good read. You can trust all SECOND CHANCE AT LOVE books to live up to the high standards of romantic fiction you've come to expect.

So happy reading, and keep your letters coming!

With warm wishes,

Ellen Edwards

Ellen Edwards
SECOND CHANCE AT LOVE
The Berkley/Jove Publishing Group
200 Madison Avenue
New York, NY 10016

Second Chance at Love

A LASTING TREASURE
CALLY HUGHES

SECOND CHANCE AT LOVE
BOOK

A LASTING TREASURE

Copyright © 1983 by Cally Hughes

Distributed by Berkley/Jove

First edition published April 1983

First printing

"Second Chance at Love" and the butterfly emblem are trademarks belonging to Jove Publications, Inc.

Printed in the United States of America

Second Chance at Love books are published by
The Berkley/Jove Publishing Group
200 Madison Avenue, New York, NY 10016

Dedicated to men—
the cause of it all.

CHAPTER ONE

"WELL, ADELINA MARY ROSE KILDAIRE"—Addy smiled at herself in the long, wide model's mirror in the dining room of the big old house—"you're doing pretty well for yourself." She plaited her wheat-colored hair into a single braid and idly considered her rounded body reflected in the mirror. How discouraging it was to have hips and breasts when one was a designer of women's clothing. Why couldn't she have been as flat as a board, like Pearl?

She heard the front door opening and closing and the hum of people talking as guests began to arrive for that afternoon's ladies-only showing of her summer line of lingerie. Gusts of frigid February air blasted into the house along with the guests, and the giant furnace in the basement rumbled into life.

1

The model's mirror was placed against the window wall. Addy looked out at the woods frozen in a tangle against the winter sky. Not for the first time, she wondered what the block had been like when all the other great houses still stood there on the north side of Indianapolis. Gradually they had been abandoned and demolished. Her own Gown House remained in lovely splendor, the single surviving house on the now-overgrown block. She owned the house, the entire block, and a staggering mortgage.

Miss Pru, her dear friend and mentor, bustled past her, hesitating long enough to scold, "You've braided your hair too tight, Addy. Your eyes are pulled back into slits. You look as if you're auditioning for *Madama Butterfly.*"

"Auditioning?" asked blond model Pattycake as she hurried in, late as usual. "Who's auditioning?" She was bursting with life, bubbly, giggly, irrepressible. She was eighteen and stagestruck.

"Addy's braid is too tight and it pulls her eyes slanted," Miss Pru explained over her shoulder as she hurried away. "She looks like Madame Butterfly."

Pattycake cocked her head and studied Addy carefully. "Your eyes are too blue," she pronounced. "You'd have to wear brown contacts. And you're really too English-looking. Your nose is too straight and your mouth is a good two inches too wide. You'd have to change all that . . . and take voice lessons."

Addy gave her a droll look and laughed, then loosened her hair and began to braid it again.

Each year she held two ladies-only shows on the afternoons before the summer and winter showings. At both the afternoon and evening shows today they would model the summer line of gowns, dresses, jackets, and raincoats. Almost one hundred people had requested tickets for one of the shows. That evening there would also be some male guests. Only the afternoon shows were restricted to women.

The hum from the drawing room grew louder, and the models rushed around getting ready. Addy surveyed the chaos and grinned. She loved it. She checked her dress in the mirror and knew it fit her well and was attractive. The long-sleeved, soft woolen shirtwaist in blue-gray made her eyes even bluer. They sparkled with excitement.

In spite of the models' nervous whispers and giggles, Addy knew everything was under control. She could easily have kept them all calm, but their excitement would communicate itself to the guests waiting out in the drawing room.

Once her braid was finished, she looped it up the back of her head and pinned it there tightly, then began to search for her daughter, three-year-old Grendel. No one ever thought she and Grendel were related, because Addy was so fair, and while Grendel was pale-cheeked, she had dark button eyes and straight black hair. She was the postage-stamp print of Paul Morris, who'd taken off when Addy had learned she was pregnant. That had left lasting scars.

Stretching to see over the models' heads, Addy called softly, "Grendel?"

"I saw her just a minute ago," offered Pearl, one of the models. She was six feet tall and incredibly thin. When she'd come to work for Addy and had said her name was Pearl, Addy had squinched up her face and asked, "Pearl?"

Pearl had just grinned and replied, in a marvelous imitation of Pearl Bailey, "Us black pearls, honey, are rare."

Pearl moved to the mirror and posed dramatically.

She wore tangerine-colored pajamas that were smashing with her chocolate skin. To Addy she said, "Aren't you glad I'm naturally this color and you didn't have to paint me in order to make the contrast between this rag and my glorious skin?"

Addy grinned and tried to pinch Pearl's nonexistent rear end. Pearl stood up straight and sent a smug look down on Addy, then snaked down a long, skinny arm and gave Addy's round bottom a sassy pat.

"You have a mean streak that wide," Addy told her. Her hands measured off two feet. "And since you're only this wide"—she put her hands about six inches apart—"you can see the over*whelming* ratio." She turned haughtily away from Pearl's grin.

"Grendel?" Addy called again. She stopped next to Miss Pru, who was making last-minute alterations on a chemise. "Have you seen Grendel?"

Miss Pru smiled indulgently and replied softly, "She's checking the house. I think she's becoming a real professional." She spoke around several pins held in her mouth, which Addy forbade *anyone* to do. But she allowed Miss Pru certain privileges. Whatever would Addy have done without her? She was middle-aged and deceptively starchy-looking, and she was all that had sustained Addy during a long, trying time.

The word "professional" made Addy pause. "Do you think it's okay for Grendel to model?" she whispered. She had been worrying about that lately.

"Of course, Addy, you know Grendel enjoys it," Miss Pru assured her in a quiet voice. "She doesn't show off as much as she shares the fun." She snipped a thread.

"Grendel's no problem," agreed redheaded Dale, who was looking contentedly at herself in the mirror.

"That's right," Pearl agreed. "She's a doll."

Addy slid her a look. "You're prejudiced," she said, which made Pearl roll her eyes at the ceiling in exasperation.

Just then Grendel hopped into the room. She skipped among the adults and grabbed Addy's hand. "Mommy," she hissed in a loud whisper, "'most every chair's tooked." Three was not known for lucid speech, Addy thought. Only those familiar with Grendel could plausibly interpret what she said.

"Taken," Addy corrected as she curled down to her child's height and pretended to straighten her gown. Grendel wore a summer nightgown of white seersucker with scattered blue flowers. It was sleeveless, with a large flounce of white eyelet around the bottom. Grendel's eyes were snapping with excitement, and Addy's heart clutched at seeing how perfect she was. It always amazed her that Grendel was real and by far the most charming and brilliant child ever born. And that wasn't just maternal prejudice, Addy assured herself. She had looked around and compared impartially.

Linda, the brunette model who was paired with Grendel whenever she modeled, also entered the room. Grendel looked like Linda's child. It made Addy almost jealous that they went so well together. Linda arranged her peignoir and bent over Grendel, checking her makeup. They both had such white skin that they needed rouge under the very strong lights to keep them from looking washed-out. Linda examined Grendel critically, added a dab more rouge on her nose and chin, and leaned back, peering at her but not frowning. Addy had reminded her often that frowns cause wrinkles.

As Pearl put it, the models were blond Pattycake, brunette Linda, redheaded Dale, and one black Pearl. The others had named Pearl as their outstanding model, and, since she was so tall, she groaned and rolled her eyes at their play on words.

Miss Pru modeled older women's clothes with elegant style, but Addy considered her own rounded figure unsuitable for modeling. While she seldom showed anything herself, she would end the afternoon session today with a lovely, subtly naughty robe.

It was time to begin the fashion show. Miss Pru started the music tapes. Addy took the contrived three steps up to the tall, curtained double doors between the dining room and the drawing room and stepped into the lights beamed on the entrance. She grinned at the women sitting on folding wooden chairs, which Pearl's father, Marcus, had borrowed from his church. Marcus was Addy's security. He could fix anything.

The runway was five feet wide and twenty feet long, contrived of planks set on sturdy trestles, with chairs on either side. The sides of the walkway were draped with cloth.

The walls of the drawing room were covered with a neutral burlap that had been pleated vertically from the chair rail to the ceiling. It would suffice until Addy could afford to have the walls replastered. It made a nice textured background for the showings. The room had been cleared of its customary furniture and rugs.

More than fifty women were present for the fashion show. All of them were customers. The first year there had been fifty women also, but thirty-eight had been friends pulled in to fill the chairs. When Addy welcomed the guests, her chatter conveyed a natural friendliness. She felt very comfortable with women. It was a snap for her to narrate the ladies-only show.

After she'd greeted the women, she stepped off the ramp to sit on a high stool placed at the left of the runway out of the spotlight. That way the guests wouldn't look at her but at the models as she described what they wore. In order to give her four models enough time to change, Addy made it a practice to describe the material, any unusual aspects of the garment, and how it was constructed. She also explained where she'd gotten the trim and material.

"Dale's panties are mostly cotton for coolness," she told the guests. "We usually use a blend from Texas or North Carolina, but this material is from Egypt. Did you know that Egypt has been exporting cotton for over two thousand years? They probably did it before then too.

"Dale's robe weighs only four ounces because the cloth is so fine. Gussets have been put under the arms so that there's enough room to reach easily without straining the fragile cloth."

Dale turned and moved, and the robe floated out like a soft, green-tinted mist. Her body looked lovely in the fine lingerie. The summer underwear and nightgowns were sheer and revealing, but the models weren't self-conscious.

It pleased Addy to hear a constant hum of comments during the showing. It was all very relaxed and informal. As usual, there was a pleased murmur for Grendel, who came out dancing and laughing, and several oohs and aahs rose from the women for some of the robes and nightwear.

For the last segment of the show, Pearl took Addy's place in order to give her time to change into the robe she would model. She disappeared through the hall rather than back over the ramp. She could hear Pearl describe her own robe. "Since this makes me look like I have a figure, you can tell Addy's a genius..."

Addy changed, made sure her hair was slicked back, discouraging the little wisps that tended to curl around the edges, and returned to the ramp in time to hear Pearl say, "And so to bed. Me, I just wear basic black." They laughed, as always. "But Adelina has something you'll like. She's going to describe it to you herself."

Addy slipped through the drapes into the lights, standing in a deceptively simple, pale peach robe. She assumed a formal, aloof pose. She wore tiny pink pearls in her ears. The robe was a soft lawn, sleeveless and fitted to the hips before it fell to the floor in soft folds. Over the shoulders and around the low-scooped neck there was a soft four-inch bias ruffle. The robe was very feminine.

Addy turned, moving slowly, showing it off. "Actually, being manless, I wear an old flannel bathrobe to bed." They tittered. She could see clearly only those women close by, because the rest of the room was in shadow. Some of the women had been her first customers, and she'd become very fond of them.

"There's braided horsehair in the bottom hem to weight it down so it'll swing nicely," she explained. She twirled around, and the skirt swung in a lovely circle.

"In the olden days," Addy went on, "Coco Chanel weighted her suit jackets with a gold chain in the hem. When you stood up or moved, the weight of the chain would straighten the jacket and keep it neat. Gold, being the price it is, is not in the hem of this robe, just the horsehair.

"Ginger Rogers once wore a weighted skirt to dance with Fred Astaire so that when she turned the skirt would wrap around her. As she paused, it would slowly unwrap. It was so heavy that it almost toppled poor Fred. He had to change his steps to stay out of reach of that heavy skirt.

"Now this skirt won't knock any man over." She looked up at her audience and grinned. "At least not by itself." They laughed. Addy turned, letting the skirt flare, then cautioned, "Don't do this on a stairway. You might really break a leg—not just in the show-biz sense."

She stood still, demure again and formal. "Now, no woman, wearing a robe like this, is going to style her hair this way." She indicated her slicked-back braid, then pulled out the pins, slid off the elastic holder, and easily unbraided her hair. She rumpled it with both hands and peered through it vaguely. "Is that more like it?" There was a chuckling murmur of agreement.

She ran her fingers through her hair, controlling it but leaving it marvelously, carelessly tousled as she continued telling them about the robe. "This material is very soft, but it's built so that it will stay up—if you want it to." She grinned a little wickedly. "If you undo this top hook"—she put her hands up to her chest and did that—"it will still stay up, but the shoulder strap tends to slide off." She showed them, allowing one strap to slide slowly down. "If you undo the second hook, both shoulder straps give up." Addy undid the hook, and both shoulder straps dropped away from her shoulders. She assumed a sweet expression, and in a hammed-up version of a Southern accent asked, "Don't I look like my name's Daisy June?

"But even with the second hook undone," she continued, "your bosom will stay covered." She showed them as she moved, turned, and leaned over. She gathered her hair at the top of her head before she said, "The third hook will bare your bosom, but," she advised, "you let him do that." She laughed with the guests as she allowed her hair to spill over her shoulders . . . and her eyes lifted to the silhouette of a man just inside the door of the entrance hall! What was *he* doing at a ladies-only show? But he *was* there. She stared. He was a powerful wedge of wide shoulders and narrow hips. His feet were apart, his fists on his lean hips, and his head was thrust forward, completing his aggressive stance.

Addy felt like a slave girl on the block exhibiting herself to bidders. The man looked as if he was about to make a bid. Her lips parted as she waited for it, and an absolutely remarkable sensual sensation ran up her thighs, through her stomach, and up into her breasts.

She blinked and jerked her head as she realized where she was. She sketched an abrupt nod at the clapping and chattering women, then whirled and stepped down through the drapes. "There's a *man* out there!" she hissed at Pearl.

"A man?" Pearl was astonished. "What's he doing here?"

"Acting as if he's in a slave market eyeing the merchandise."

"Watch yo mouf, white chile."

Indignant, Addy huffed, "Pearl, blacks aren't the only ones who've been slaves. Why, right this minute in—"

"Calm yourself, Addy, I'll call Papa." Pearl hurried away as Miss Pru bustled out front.

Addy snatched up her blue woolen shirtwaist and clutched it to her chest like a shield. He'd watched her do all that. Who was he? "Pattycake," Addy whispered, "go see if he's still there." She fumbled out of the robe and jerked the blue wool dress over hear head.

Pattycake sighed with exasperation. "Okay, okay! But it's not as if you were *exposed* or anything!" She went off, not over the steps via the runway but around through the hall.

Addy raked back her hair, furiously braiding it skin-tight. Her cheeks were hot. Was she blushing? She hadn't blushed since she'd told her family about Grendel. Twenty-seven, an unmarried mother, and she could still blush? How weird. Why would she blush? It had to be anger. Why was she angry?

She'd been fully dressed, but she hadn't expected a

man to be at the lingerie showing. She must be feeling hostile because he'd watched her as she'd moved, and he'd listened to what she'd said. She'd acted out of character because she'd been sure there were only women present. Women say things to other women they'd never say to men, she reasoned. If she'd known he was going to be around, she'd never have modeled that robe at all!

She fidgeted, waiting for Pattycake to return. For some reason she really didn't want to face that man—not after the way she'd behaved up on the runway. Thinking of him as he watched her up there, she felt a strange sensation touch her stomach again. She'd never felt that way before. What was it?

Standing in the doorway, he'd looked so . . . formidable, as if he'd carelessly pay the asked price, whatever it was. She shivered a little, but she wasn't cold, and the shiver wasn't from fear. It was more as if she was . . . excited.

She reminded herself that she was a grown woman. She could handle anything. She'd been on her own and self-supporting since she'd first gone to college. She'd worked at every kind of honest work she could find, and she'd survived. She'd survived it all.

She stared out the window at the gloomy winter snow and frowned. Why was she reluctant to face him? Of course, with Miss Pru and Marcus to protect her, she hadn't had to deal with any man except in the most casual way. She didn't have the leisure time for a full social life, and she didn't really miss it. She'd dated enough to know men weren't important to her. She loved her work, Grendel, her house, Miss Pru, and all the rest. She didn't need some man moving in and disrupting the careful balance. Moving in? What did she mean by assuming he wanted to move in? Other than standing militantly in the door, what exactly had he done? She tried to decide.

Pattycake came back and said, "He's gone." She sounded disappointed.

"Good."

"But he's coming back tonight. He got some tickets from Miss Pru for his mother."

"We don't have any left!" Addy objected. "How could she give him tickets?"

Pattycake raised her eyebrows and said with slow emphasis, "His mother is Elizabeth Turner Harrow."

Addy eyed her excited face. "What's that supposed to mean?"

"You're obviously not an Indy native."

"Is anyone?" Addy asked.

"Elizabeth Turner Harrow is a civic leader."

"Hooray for her."

"Now, Addy, she's a very nice lady. And she's also involved in the theater!"

"Ahhhhh." Now Addy understood. Pattycake had theatrical ambitions. "So you're going to do Little Nell on the runway tonight?"

Pattycake's eyes danced. "I'd considered Lady Macbeth."

"Of course, the Scots tartan," Addy guessed, naming a summer dress to be modeled that evening.

"But I decided that's been overdone." Pattycake posed, arm out, head thrown back.

"It's generally underdone—as in half-baked," Addy remarked dryly.

"So I thought Blanche from *Streetcar* would do it."

Addy nodded in understanding. "The smoke-gray chiffon evening dress."

"Umm-hmm. It's perfect." She fell into the role, deliberately awful. "Oh Stanley you beast."

"I don't remember that line."

"I'm improvising." Pattycake gave an excessively sweet, eyelash-fluttering smile.

"Don't."

She grinned naturally. "I wouldn't."

"Thank God."

"But I was tempted!"

As Addy groaned, Pattycake commented with eighteen-year-old tolerance, "Oh, Ad, you're so easy to tease. You take everything so seriously. You didn't think I'd *really*—"

"Nothing people your age does surprises people of my age."

"I'll find your cane," Pattycake promised as she flitted away.

That left Addy free of distraction, and her thoughts of the man came winging back. He was very attractive. But she hadn't really seen him. How could she find him attractive and so distracting? He'd be there that very night. And he'd be watching. Why would he care one way or the other? He wouldn't. But if he did come back that evening there she'd be, doing the narration.

Of course, she wouldn't be looking at the guests. She'd be sitting in the shadows to the side, looking at the models. Even if he glanced at her, there'd be nothing to hold his attention. It was no big deal. Why was her silly mind running around that way?

But as soon as everyone left, Addy cornered Miss Pru and went to some lengths to coerce her into doing the narration that evening. "That's perfectly silly, Adelina," Miss Pru protested. "You've practiced it and know it all by heart. I'd have to read it."

"Practice now," Addy coaxed.

Miss Pru scowled at her. "Why can't you do it?"

"My throat's gone." Addy choked a little. "It's very sore."

"Let me see."

"Stay away! You might get it too." Addy backed away.

"You're acting very strange." Miss Pru assessed her, frowning. "I've never seen you like this. What's the matter?"

"My throat," Addy croaked, raising a protective hand to it.

"Nonsense!" Miss Pru studied Addy with narrowed eyes. "That man this afternoon, Dr. Samuel Grady..."

"Samuel Grady? That's who that was?" Addy's hand dropped from her throat, and her voice sounded perfectly normal. "Who's Samuel Grady?"

"He's a consultant for pediatricians," Miss Pru answered, a knowing look coming into her eyes.

"How do you know that?"

"He gave me his card when I asked him what he was doing here," Miss Pru explained.

"Why *was* he here?"

"To pick up tickets for tonight's show for his mother."

"We didn't have any more. How'd you find any? Where would we put anyone else?"

"I gave him five." Miss Pru began to needlessly straighten dresses hanging on nearby racks.

"Is the chandelier going to hold five more people?" Addy gestured wildly.

Miss Pru wasn't worried. "Marcus will find a way."

"Where's the card?" Addy wanted to see it.

"In your office." Addy started to hurry away, but Miss Pru laid a hand on her arm to stop her and added shrewdly, "Is it because he's coming back tonight? Is that why you don't want to do the narration?"

"No, no!" Addy made her voice husky. "It's my throat. Do you think for one minute I'd let some man boggle me?"

Miss Pru didn't reply, but Addy could see from the way she tightened her lips that she had to bite her tongue to keep from saying more.

CHAPTER TWO

WHEN THE AFTERNOON ladies finally drifted away they left behind a very nice number of orders, enough to give cause for high glee. Addy's response, however, was somewhat subdued by the thought of Dr. Samuel Grady's imminent return. She shooed Grendel and the chattering models upstairs to various rooms to rest before the evening show at six. Then she went to her own room.

Instead of lying down, she stood at the window thinking. Sometimes she thought the shows every three months were too much for them. Not for the models so much as for the seamstresses—and for Marcus and his crew. She knew she was lucky that the models were so accommodating, and she appreciated it.

Things were looking up, she thought as she gazed down at the snow-covered yard. Not very far up yet, but up. The overhead was staggering. The inventory of materials and equipment in that barn of a house was vital. Her four full-time seamstresses were jewels and worked very hard. It also helped to have several other women who did piecework at their homes—gussets, zippers, and the tab fronts of shirts.

And thank God for Marcus, Pearl's very large father. He'd volunteered his help when they'd first moved into the house. He could be dictatorial, but he kept her car going and the ancient furnace in the basement rumbling. How could she keep the sewing machines going without him? He was a magician when it came to motors—or to convincing someone they wanted to leave her property. He was intimidatingly huge. Next to Marcus, Pearl looked like a munchkin!

How old was Marcus? She knew he'd been married several times. Hedda was Pearl's stepmother. Addy speculated on what had happened to his other wives and wondered if Hedda might have hurried along her predecessor. Hedda looked as if she could do something like that.

Then there was the house. Addy touched the peeling paint on the windowsill. It constantly needed care. She was forever getting notes saying she owed Marcus for some repair. She called it blackmail. "Why don't I just turn all my income over to you and you give me what's left!" she often told him.

"Don't get biggity," he always said loftily.

"Biggity?" she huffed. "Me?"

"Your grammar's dreadful," he would reply.

She looked around her room. Of course, in that old house, with twenty-four rooms—counting the four in the attic—there was bound to be something going wrong all the time. Then, too, Marcus charged her a hundred dollars a month for "grounds upkeep." With the help of his ever-changing team of young, otherwise unemployed men, the walks were shoveled in winter, the grass mowed in summer, and the gravel drive kept weeded and raked. "Marcus, why don't we get a rider-mower?" she'd asked. "It could be converted in winter to a snowplow, and we'd save money in the long run."

Marcus had barely acknowledged her as he'd directed a young man to trim around the curbs of the basement window wells. "No," he said, "the young men need something to do."

There just wasn't any answer to that, and Addy had to admit they did a good job. Her block always looked well-kept.

Then one day Marcus had brought a sleepy-eyed, shyly smiling young black girl named Emmaline to the Gown House. "You need another seamstress," he told Addy.

Addy resisted. "Well, not right now."

"You can pay her by the piece—while she's learning," Marcus had pronounced.

Miss Pru had put Emmaline to work. Addy had huffed, "I don't know why I'm even consulted! Everyone does exactly as *he* wants to around here!" But Miss Pru had ignored her.

Later she'd told Marcus, "Emmaline isn't a seamstress, she's a sore thumb! She does half the work of the others in twice the time. She's useless!"

Marcus stopped barely long enough to reply, "She still has to find herself."

"Emmaline wouldn't know where to start looking!" Addy snapped. "She's a dreamer. She isn't in touch with reality."

"Now, now." That was the closest Marcus had ever come to placating her. "Don't worry. Emmaline will work out."

"Work out?" Addy sputtered. "She isn't familiar enough with the word 'work' to make use of it!"

After that Addy privately called Marcus the Godfather. Not her godfather, but everybody *else*'s godfather. The Godfather of the Black Mafia.

Of course, without Marcus and Miss Pru, she would never have made it. She knew that full well. And she knew Marcus was scrupulously fair. He didn't do anything that didn't need to be done, and he charged very reasonably.

His men had painted her house. She'd instructed that it was to be white, and Marcus had nodded at her directions—then painted it antique-blue with a French-vanilla trim. "But I wanted it white!" Addy had been outraged.

"Come over here." Marcus lumbered off across the yard and across the street with her trailing along, waving her arms and objecting. He'd ignored her, then turned and gestured. "See? It's just right." Not waiting for her reaction, he'd started back. She'd seen that he was right. That was the most frustrating thing about Marcus: he was always right.

When they'd had their first show Marcus had said, "My wife, Hedda, will do the catering."

Addy had replied politely, "Thanks, but Miss Pru and I will do that."

"No," he'd said. "You'll be too busy. The afternoon ladies want something dainty and sweet, and the evening bunch will want something different. Hedda will fix it."

"But, Marcus . . ."

"It's the eats what makes the product look good."

"The . . . eats?" She couldn't believe she'd heard right.

"Don't sass," he advised. —

"How can you criticize my grammar, then come up with 'eats'?"

"Watch yo mouf."

"Good grief!" She'd laughed. Then she'd looked at him, getting serious, and said, "You know, Marcus, you could make a fortune fixing motors."

"I do," he told her. "You need another sewing machine. You need a backup. A couple of them are running on my genius alone, and even genius can't keep metal from wearing."

"Why don't we set you up a repair shop in the basement? You'd make a bundle."

"People who get things fixed that way are either very poor or very rich, but rich people who are that frugal don't buy designer clothes. It's a different clientele entirely, and not what you want."

"I worry about the time you have to spend on my things and how many people you find work for, but I don't figure you get any of it. You give it all away."

"I have sufficient income," he assured her.

"From 'eats' to 'sufficient income'?"

"Hedda will do the eats."

And Hedda had and still did. She was magnificent, large, but not large in a fat way. She was simply a tall, magnificent woman. Her skin was very black, and her lips were black too, and perfectly formed. Her eyes were very white with ink-black irises. She was intimidating. She rarely smiled, but when she did it knocked you backward. And she never spoke. If Addy or Miss Pru said something to her, she listened and either shrugged, nodded, or shook her head.

Hedda was a magician when it came to food. The tea cakes for the afternoon showings were traditional English fare, but her hors d'oeuvres were imaginative and delicious. Once Addy had told Hedda, "I don't know if they come for the showing, or if they come for your hors d'oeuvres and stay for the showing to be polite." And Hedda had nodded.

Hedda wore African, or quasi-African, dress. It was really Hedda dress, and it was so exotic that on anyone else it would have seemed ostentatious. It looked right on Hedda. With her nodded permission, Addy had copied a brown and cream version of Hedda's wiggles and dots and stripes to make a summer cloth that had been very popular.

Addy knew that fabric design could make or break a dress, as could trim. The wilder the print, the simpler the dress should be. When she did her own designs, she signed them. She'd had several extremely successful simple summer dresses that were perfect because of their unusual fabric.

When Addy worked in the attic with waxes, pots, and color baths, Emmaline would sometimes lean against the doorway and watch. She drove the busy, driven Addy to frustrated distraction. Addy would shoo Emmaline back to her sewing machine. To Addy, Emmaline was a zero. Pearl and Heda were worth every cent, but that Emmaline kept turning up like a bad penny.

Addy was distracted from her thoughts when Miss Pru came into the room and scolded, "Why aren't you lying down?"

"I'm not tired," Addy protested before she remembered her fragile throat.

"Lie down," Miss Pru commanded. "I have a vinegar cloth to put on that throat."

"I don't want a vinegar cloth on my throat. It won't do any good. Vinegar cloths are supposed to help headaches." But she lay down anyway, and Miss Pru put the cloth on her throat, patted her cheek, and left the room.

Addy lay there grimly with a vinegar cloth on her non-sore throat and considered how Miss Pru, Marcus, and Hedda ordered her around. She decided the reason the strange man worried her was that he might try to pry away her last vestige of independence. But why would he want to do that, and what independence did she still have? She faced the reality: she had none. She'd lost control of her whole life. What in the world was she doing lying there in bed with a vinegar cloth on her throat?

She removed the cloth and tip toed up to the attic to fiddle with the silk-screen frame, which had loosened, hoping not to run into Miss Pru or Hedda. From the top of the grand staircase she had heard Miss Pru rehearsing the evening's narration. Addy practiced subtle coughs from her unscratchy throat. Life was sometimes very demanding.

A while later, Grendel scrambled up the attic stairs, having awoken from her nap. *"Mommy!"* she greeted her mother with great joy. Who could resist? They woke up the models, and all of them trooped down to the kitchen for a light snack of Hedda's perfect hors d'oeuvres. Then the models went about making sure their changes were in the right sequence for the narration. Addy could tell that Miss Pru had the narration down pat. Addy had been trying to mimic the silent Hedda and limit her conversation to head nods and shakes to disguise her normal throat, but she was distracted by the thought of seeing Sam Grady, pediatric consultant, and every once in a while a word slipped out.

Would he come? Maybe he'd just taken enough tickets to give to his mother, Elizabeth Turner Harrow. If she was his mother, why wasn't there a Grady in her name? If he didn't show up, Addy would have wasted a lot of trouble getting out of doing the narration.

Listening to the front door opening for the first of the

guests, she was very surprised to realize she'd be a little let down if he didn't show up. She fidgeted and paced around needlessly and listened as the crowd gathered. Would he come?

He did. He and an older woman and three younger ones finally arrived. Addy glimpsed him discussing the hors d'oeuvres with them. He smiled and licked his fine lips discreetly and turned his handsome head, which was set on a strong throat atop wide shoulders that led down to a perfect, muscular body that was selfishly concealed from view by an extremely expensive and well-fitted suit. What a show-off he was, standing there quietly, speaking inaudibly, and drawing every feminine eye to himself. . . .

What in God's name was the matter with her? She was antimale and had been for four years. She never wanted anything more to do with another man. She was completely immune, not only to males, but to male doctors who were pediatric consultants. She was a mature, independent woman, pursuing a fine career and in control of her own life. Anyway, those three young women didn't look like Sam or each other, so they couldn't be his sisters. One or all three of them must be his wife, ex-wife or mistress.

"I'll do the narration," Addy told Miss Pru coolly.

"Your throat's all right again?" The question was so placid that Addy lifted her chin when she replied that it was.

"It must have been the vinegar cloth," Miss Pru said smugly.

Ignoring her, Addy walked deliberately past Dr. Samuel Grady, but she did it very quickly, as if she was in a hurry, and when she was sure his back would be to her. When she was past them, she turned and nodded politely, giving his group a slight smile, although her eyes didn't focus on anyone. Even unfocused, he was devastating. Her stomach quivered and her thighs tingled.

How on earth could she feel such a reaction to a man she'd never really looked at? He was probably actually ugly. She was building all this up impossibly. Three glimpses of a man and her silly mind had woven a romantic version of Sir Galahad. What did she know about him? He had a great silhouette. He was excessively masculine in impact. He was a pediatric consultant, and he had a mother. Lots of doctors had mothers. The whole thing was ridiculous. If she got a good, clear look at him, she'd be disillusioned. She turned at the end of the room, stood still, and focused deliberately on him.

He was watching her. He smiled just a little and looked amused. She'd been wrong. He wasn't devastating, he was ruinously gorgeous. Not gorgeous meaning beautiful, but a gorgeous, rugged male.

She flitted blindly away and left the room by instinct. She told herself that in spite of his deep, pleasant voice he probably had a high-pitched giggle. Then in the hum of the crowd she heard the rumble of a man's laugh and knew in her bones it was him.

Gradually the guests filtered into the drawing room and sat down still chatting. An air of hushed anticipation settled over the room, and Addy found that her palms were wet with perspiration. What a relief that she knew the narration by heart. Her thoughts were winging away in all directions. When the crowd laughed at her patter, she was startled.

Pearl had the temerity to lean over from the runway and suggest with a flared-eyed snarl that she slow down a little. Addy thought Pearl would turn out to be just like Marcus. With Hedda for a stepmother and Marcus for a father, what chance did Pearl have of being docile? Addy's mind went spiraling along, but her mouth did slow down, giving the models a little more time to change.

After the showing, the guests seemed to linger longer than usual. Everyone appeared to know Elizabeth Turner Harrow, and apparently she was in no hurry to leave, so there was nice, leisurely visiting. Mrs. Harrow kept the general conversation on the show and the materials, and she ordered two dresses, a suit, and a raincoat. She chose a thin, flowered material in delicate colors for the raincoat and asked for an umbrella to match. Addy accepted the order without a flicker of an eyelash. She'd never made an umbrella before, but she'd figure out how. She could always buy one and recover it. Was that legal?

Addy smiled rather tightly as she took orders from the three younger women and set up the dates for their fittings. That their names were all different only made it more reasonable that they were all Sam's great and good friends. She noticed he was easy and familiar with them in an intimately teasing way that suggested long acquaintance.

Busy as she was, Addy still managed to study all three women. They were very smooth and good-looking. They'd lived pampered, untroubled, proper lives that were well-spent, not frittered away. They were so confident and comfortable with themselves that Addy's mouth went a little sour.

A quick glance showed her that other women were leaving orders with the models and Miss Pru, and Grendel was grinning and being darling as she stood by one or another of her "family."

Just then, next to Addy's ear, his deep voice light and silky, Sam said, "So she's your daughter?"

Addy nodded stiffly. "Grendel." She stared no higher than his perfectly made lapel.

"Grendel?" Humor laced the name as he said it.

She shot him a hostile glance. "Yes."

"You look like the Grendel; she looks like an Addy."

Thrills went through her at hearing him say her name, and she examined her thumbnail, finding it fascinating, then said primly, "We like our names."

"I do too. Where is . . . Mr. Kildaire?"

She decided he might as well know. "I'm not married."

"That's nice to hear."

Nice? When she considered all the agony not being married had brought her? Nice wasn't a very good word. . . .

"Grendel looks like a healthy little girl." He made the observation in a friendly way.

"Do you always consider a child's health?" she asked in a less friendly way.

"Don't you look at clothes?"

She glanced up briefly and smiled just a bit as she admitted, "Yes." He grinned down at her, his eyes still amused, and sensation washed through her, taking all the starch out of her body, leaving it weakened, softened, and not too reliable.

Mrs. Harrow approached them and said she must be going. "I'm already late for a meeting, but they'll be so slow getting started, making coffee and gossiping, that I'll still make the important part of the evening's business." She exchanged a smile with Addy, then asked, "If I gathered fifty women, would you arrange another showing?"

Still feeling weak, Addy found the offer stunning. A dream! "Oh, yes!" she said.

"May I call you about the day?" Mrs. Harrow asked kindly. "It would be all right?"

"Oh, yes. I'd love to." Addy frowned a little.

"I know how tight your time must be," Mrs. Harrow apologized, "but I have some friends who simply must see your show. You're a very clever designer, and your things are lovely."

"Oh, it's no problem," Addy hastened to reassure her. "I was frowning because I ended the sentence with part of an infinitive and Marcus..."

"Marcus?" Sam questioned, scowling. "Who's Marcus?"

Mrs. Harrow's grin was exactly like her son's teasing one as she asked, "Now why would that worry you?"

Addy ignored Sam's question and laughed with Mrs. Harrow. As the three young women who'd come with them walked over, Sam touched Addy's elbow and said, "I'll be seeing you." She managed to give him a quick glance as Mrs. Harrow shook her hand.

The three women claimed Addy's attention. One said, "Your designs are just marvelous."

Another said, "I'm so glad we could get tickets. It was an excellent show—and so well done."

The third exclaimed, "How did you ever get Hedda Freeman to cater?" When Addy gave her a blank look, the woman grinned and said, "You must have clout. Hedda quit catering five years ago."

The three women had to relinquish Addy's attention as other people came up to say good-bye and comment on the show, but Addy was distracted. Sam had left, and she felt blank.

She wasn't aware of all the others leaving, but eventually she looked up and found they had gone. She glanced around the empty rooms and noted that Miss Pru was turning off the lights. She helped, then followed her up the stairs and murmured good night.

Not paying any real attention, she automatically prepared for bed, climbed in, stretched out, and gave herself over to her thoughts. The evening had had a different flavor, and she decided it was because Mrs. Harrow was such a vivacious woman. She was Samuel Grady's mother and a little awesome. Handsome, too. She would be a terrific advertisement for Adelina Kildaire's clothes. People would ask her where she had found that dress or suit, and Mrs. Harrow would say, "At the Gown House." She was a gracious lady, and she was Sam's mother.

Addy allowed herself to consider Sam. He was being obviously friendly and interested. Well, it wouldn't do him any good. She was through with men forever. She'd slept with a man, and she hadn't liked it at all. It had been painful and embarrassing. She never wanted to go through that again. And she wouldn't have to, because she had Grendel. There was no reason to have anything else to do with any man. And that included Samuel Grady, M.D.

CHAPTER THREE

JUST TWO REASONABLY normal days later Miss Pru came
to Addy in her workroom and said, "Dr. Grady is out in
the reception room and wants to see the robe you modeled
during the lingerie show."

"Oh? Ask someone else." Addy went back to work.

"There *is* no one else." Miss Pru was patient.

"Isn't anyone here?"

"If anyone was, would I say there was no one else?"

Addy was intrigued by the expression on Miss Pru's
face. It was a quizzing kind of look. Addy would have
liked to spend some time exploring why Miss Pru should
look that particular way, but she was too boggled by the
prospect of seeing Samuel Grady again. "You do it," she
told Miss Pru.

Miss Pru huffed in an incredulous way and snapped, "Don't be ridiculous!" She left the room.

Addy looked down at herself and decided the sweater she was wearing was too snug over her chest. She ran upstairs and put on a starched, mud-colored shirtwaist with a cream neck scarf and added high heels so she'd be less intimidated by Sam's height. Then, looking into the mirror, she skinned back her hair into its stern braid.

But her attempt at disguise wasn't successful. The dress was actually very flattering, even though it was mud-colored. It was nipped in to show off her waist, and the skirt flared out over her hips, drawing attention to her legs. Nervousness made her cheeks pink and her lips red.

Breathing deeply to steady herself, she walked down the grand staircase in a stately, businesslike manner. Then, carrying the robe, she walked into the reception room. The runway had been removed and the customary furniture and rugs had been replaced. She nodded to acknowledge Sam, although she didn't really focus on him.

The power of his attraction made her hands fumble, and she licked her lips and swallowed. Then he said good morning, and her eyes couldn't settle on anything.

By being very formal, maybe she could overcome her nervous reaction to him. "You wanted to see this robe, sir?"

"Very much."

"Here." She thrust it toward him.

"Well, since I'm not sure I saw it properly, I would like to see it modeled." He paused when she said nothing, then added, "May I?"

"I'm sorry. None of the models is here right now."

"Couldn't . . . you?" Was that amusement in his silky voice?

"Well, you see ... I ... uh ..."

"Please?" His voice deepened and softened.

My God, she thought, and knew those three women must be his slaves. They probably wouldn't even mind that sex was revolting and messy just so long as it pleased him. She wondered which one was the favorite who was going to be gifted with that robe.

Filled with a turmoil she didn't understand but, even more incredible, filled with a need for him to see her in that robe again, she nodded brusquely and went through the house to a dressing room. She'd been oblivious to the women working there before. She changed into the robe, tossing her freshly starched dress into a heap.

She didn't have the courage to take down her hair, but she took off her shoes and made her way back to him barefooted. Her palms were wet, her lips dry, and her tongue was stuck to the roof of her mouth.

Halfway back through the big rooms, she said to herself, What are you doing, Adelina Mary Rose Kildaire? Just what *are* you doing? She stopped to consider her conduct. Then she hunted out Grendel and took her hand and walked sedately back to Dr. Samuel Grady, with a three-year-old child as protection.

Addy stopped just inside the draped double door, clutching Grendel's hand with both of hers, staring at Sam's chest. Grendel balanced on one foot, her other foot on her knee. She examined Dr. Grady with a lively expression and beamed a smile at him, which he returned. Addy thought that her eyes couldn't be totally useless if she could see all that.

Sam said to Addy, "Could you ... uh ... turn?" He stood watching with great interest, drawing a circle with his hand to show her what he meant.

She nodded and released Grendel's hand as if it were her first time on ice skates and she was being forced to release the rail that had been supporting her. Stiff as a poker, she walked forward, turned, and walked back to where she'd been. She picked up Grendel's hand again. Grendel blinked up at her, squirmed her hand free, hopped over to a table, and disappeared under it.

Sam said, "Lovely," in a way that sent prickles down Addy's back. And then he approached and walked slowly around her, examining the robe—and her—in such a way that Addy was reminded of the first time she'd seen him. Her feeling then, of being on an auction block, flooded her senses in an alarming way.

Sam um-hmmed a couple of times, then said, "I believe there are . . . some hooks?"

Addy's hands slapped instantly against her décolletage as if she'd concealed her life's savings there and he was pointing a gun at her. She said something that resembled "Awwk." The blood drained out of her face and thrills shot up her body at the thought of him fumbling with the hooks nestled between her breasts.

He loved it. She sneaked a peek and saw sparkling humor in his eyes and a quirking of his lips. He raised his brows and said again, "The hooks?" He waited.

"This is . . . the only model." She'd had to swallow between the words.

"Just the first two," he suggested.

Addy knew any woman who wasn't as antimale as she was would have been winding around him like a cat in heat and inviting him to undo all the hooks. She was proud she'd resisted and felt very pleased with her strength of character.

He lifted his hands as if to help, but she took a long step backward, smack into the wall. Trapped there, red-faced, and acting like a high school girl with her first college man, she bent her head and carefully undid the first hook. The shoulder strap slid down slowly in a very wanton way. Her face went scarlet. Why had she ever devised this wretched thing? She took a deep breath to say the gown wasn't for sale after all.

"Very nice," Sam murmured, his voice vibrating in the pit of her body. "And the second?" He appeared to expect her to continue.

Mindlessly, her obedient hands went to the second hook. They automatically undid it, and both straps went down. Sam stepped back and just looked at her. She was standing against the wall, her arms straight down at her sides, the palms of her hands pressed against the burlap surface, her breath held.

"I'll take it."

He sounded as reasonable as if he were buying a car, but the incident brought back the runway episode with its impression of a slave market, and Addy wasn't sure if he meant he'd take the robe . . . or her.

"May I take it with me?"

So he *did* mean the robe. "Don't you want one made to . . . her specifications?" Why was that so hard to say? "Another color?" she added lamely.

"This is perfect."

"But I've worn it. At least let it be cleaned."

"I'll do that. I haven't time to come back, and later it might be gone."

Was he going to give it to . . . her . . . today? A black depression descended over Addy like a cloud. He asked the price, and she added half again as much, explaining, "Since it's been worn," as if she was cutting the cost.

"That's all?" he asked. He seemed surprised.

She clamped her teeth together and wished she'd doubled it. She flipped aside the drapes, undid the robe en route, and called for one of the women to box it as she stepped out of it and tossed it aside.

"Box it? But it's been worn!" the woman protested.

"Just go ahead and box it!" Addy said through gritted teeth.

The woman frowned, then shrugged and obeyed.

Dressed in the crumpled shirtwaist she'd retrieved from a heap on the floor, Addy smoothed her hair, grimly put on the high-heeled shoes, and went back to accept Dr. Grady's check.

He was squatted down with Grendel standing between his knees. Her tiny hands rested on his gray-suited forearms, and she was laughing with him. At first Addy was only fleetingly conscious that Grendel lived in a female world and must miss not ever being around men. Then slowly her consciousness was drawn to how alike they were—their coloring, their grins, their humor. The only dissimilar thing was their skin. His was tanned, while hers was delicately white. How strange that Grendel would look so much like a total stranger. Samuel Grady was nothing like her father.

Addy plopped the boxed robe down on a nearby table, and picked up his check. She held it up as if to verify the amount and signature, but her eyes were blind to it.

Sam rose effortlessly from his squatting position. Good leg muscles there. "I appreciate your showing me the robe," he said. "That was very kind."

"I sell clothes," she said tersely.

He smiled, appearing relaxed as he asked, "I wonder if you and Grendel and Miss Pru would be my guests for an early dinner on Friday."

Addy took three breaths, her lips parting each time, but no sound came as she looked at him, round-eyed and unbelieving. He'd asked her to dinner!

Grendel bounded around and exclaimed, "Yes!"

Addy's eyes were pulled to the movement, and her tongue stumbled awkwardly as she said, "Well..." There was no way in this world she was going to get tangled up with a man like Samuel Grady. If you walk on the track, you get hit by the train. Finally she managed to reply, "I'm afraid we have other plans for Friday."

"Oh." He looked at her kindly, but his smile faded in his obvious disappointment. "Well, perhaps another time?"

Grendel scowled and demanded in the way of children, "We can't? Why not?"

Her mother looked down at her, wishing her as silent as Hedda, and said, "Perhaps another time." As she said that, she realized she'd echoed Sam's words. It sounded as if she were agreeing to the idea.

Very smoothly he suggested, "We could go sledding on Sunday." That was a calculated offer, Addy decided. As he'd probably known she would, Grendel squealed in agreement. He cast a smugly confident look at Addy and asked, "Sunday, then? How about late morning, then having lunch?"

"Well..."

"Oh, *yes!*" squealed Grendel. "Please!" She hopped around and clapped her tiny hands.

How could she deny Grendel the outing? For Grendel, Addy would do it...once. "All right." Again she was stiff and ungracious. He'd get discouraged.

"Fine." He grinned. "I'll pick you up about ten thirty?"

Addy gave a short nod, aware that Grendel had to skip around in order to get rid of her excess excitement. "When's Sunday?" she wanted to know.

"In five days."

Grendel stopped dead and her face fell as she exclaimed in disbelief, "Five?"

Yes, lots of things could happen in five days, Addy thought, and then they wouldn't be able to go. She watched Sam pick up the box containing the robe.

To Grendel he said encouragingly, "Only five days.

And it'll be worth the wait." His glance slid back to Addy.

"Five?" Grendel said again and made her little face look pitiful.

"Cut it out, Grendel," Addy warned. God knew where she got her dramatics. "Say, 'I shall look forward to it, Dr. Grady.'"

"You a doctor?" Grendel asked.

"Yes."

"Like *my* doctor Je-wam-ee Tin-keh?"

"Oh, is Jeremy Tinker your doctor?" He lifted his eyebrows in question to Addy. She didn't reply but she didn't deny it, and Sam said, "I was in medical school with him. He's a good friend and a fine doctor."

"He makes faces," Grendel supplied.

"Faces?"

She nodded seriously. "When I get a shot. He make terrible face. Once I cry"—her tiny, mobile face looked very pathetic—"he howl. Like a dog."

"That's good old Jeremy all right." Sam bit his lip and added, "He has wolf blood."

Sam escaped while Addy was trying to explain that to Grendel.

On Saturday Grendel awoke with a 104-degree fever. Addy reported it to Dr. Tinker's answering service. It shouldn't have been such a surprise when Dr. Samuel Grady, pediatric consultant, turned up at the Gown House. But it was.

"What are you doing here?" Addy asked in astonishment as she let him in the front door. "Do you make house calls?" She glanced at him as they went upstairs to Grendel's room.

"I'm taking some of Jeremy's calls this weekend," he replied smoothly. "And I was going right by here"—he grinned at Grendel—"so I decided I'd best see why my sledding partner was lying around in bed and not feeling very well." His eyes turned to Addy in such an accusing way that she wondered if he suspected her of deliberately making her child sick in order to avoid going out with him.

Grendel obviously felt so rotten that she didn't have to pretend, as Addy knew she did on occasion. Sam stayed with her for an hour, sponging her off and sympathizing with her while he gave her a shot to stop her nausea. Watching him, Addy decided he must have majored in bedside. She squirmed uncomfortably, appalled to realize she was envious of the concentrated attention Grendel was getting from Sam. Grendel felt too poorly to appreciate it, Addy was sure. When Grendel was really sick she was a sober, cooperative, uncomplaining patient, like now. It scared the living daylights out of Addy.

After the hour was up, Sam said he'd be back later, which made a gelatin mass of Addy, who followed him down the stairs on ramshackle legs. "Is she that sick that you have to come back?" she asked anxiously.

"Oh, no! Why did you think that?" He sounded surprised.

"Well, to have to come back here, and I thought, with you being a consultant and all, that she must be..."

"No, no, no." He shook his head. "I'm at loose ends, and I'll be in the area a little later, so I'll stop in just to see how she's getting along."

"And she isn't dying or anything?" Addy's chin quivered.

"No, she's fine." He peered at her. "Are you all right?" He felt her head. "Open your mouth."

She complied automatically, until she realized what she was doing and snapped it closed, then said shortly, "I'm too old for you."

"No," he denied, "you're just about right."

"Are you implying I'm a child? Childish?" she said a little huffily.

But he only chuckled. He shrugged into his coat, picked up his bag, and opened the door. "Don't give her anything by mouth until I come back." He started out, then turned back. "Unless I'm longer than four hours. In that case give her a little weak, sweetened tea, a tablespoon at a time."

Addy said, "Yes," then added automatically, "Thank you for coming."

He only grinned again and left. She watched him go surefooted down the icy steps and out to his car. She wondered who had gotten the robe and how he'd shown her about the hooks. The thought made an odd, powerful twist go through her. She tried to figure out why she was so depressed and thought it must be that Grendel was feeling so awful. Poor baby.

Almost two hours to the minute, Sam Grady returned. He brought Grendel a box of green Popsicles. He mashed one up in a bowl and fed it to her with a spoon. She watched him with big, sad eyes and complained because she wouldn't be able to go sledding the next day. She even managed to squeeze out a tear in such a way that Addy was cheered. Grendel's being so dramatic had to mean she was getting better.

By then it was approaching dinnertime, and the delicious aroma of Miss Pru's roast beef and hot bread was wafting up the back stairway, mouth-wateringly seductive. If Grendel was good at drama, Sam was no piker. He straightened his back wearily, inhaling deeply with great appreciation while he said woefully, "That certainly smells good." He made it sound as if his nose were pressed against the outside of a windowpane as he stood barefooted in the snow.

What could Addy do? She was trapped. He'd come to see Grendel twice. Even though she dreaded his bill, she was grateful he'd been there. So she asked, however reluctantly, "You wouldn't want to stay to dinner, would you?" It wasn't even a question, just a negative statement, accompanied by a shaking of her head. It was as left-footed an offer as possible, and she expected him to refuse it.

"Why, how nice of you!" he exclaimed, doing a good job of sounding surprised. "It's terrible to be a bachelor, because my apartment is never filled with the fragrance of home cooking. It's a cold, impersonal place I just use to store my things and to sleep in a cold bed."

"That's too much, you saying that so pitifully," she scoffed.

"I thought I'd done that quite well!" he replied with asperity. "I got invited to dinner, didn't I?"

"If you want a home life and home cooking, you can get married, or hire a cook."

"I'm working on it."

Her stomach clutched at his words. Was he . . . courting someone? Would he marry someone? "Where do you live?" she asked.

"I'm staying at Windridge. I've a condo there. Do you know it? It's on Emmerson off Fall Creek, about five miles east of Meridian Hills. It's very attractive, but you have no idea how much a home-cooked meal can mean to a bachelor."

Addy suspected she'd just been maneuvered. She narrowed her eyes and studied him. He was tricky. She'd have to be very careful. She watched him perk up as if he were a new puppy just adopted, and he and Grendel chuckled and chatted. He was tricky all right, and she had just better watch her step.

CHAPTER FOUR

GRENDEL SAID HER tummy wasn't hungry for a meal, so after Sam promised her another Popsicle in an hour, he and Addy went downstairs to help Miss Pru. Miss Pru smiled a welcome at Sam and scurried about her work. She was sixty-three and looked forty-eight. She tinted her hair in a clever way, her figure was excellent, and, although her lips were thin and seemed prim, her smile was wide and friendly.

Miss Pru handed them platters and bowls for the table. The back hall, beyond the kitchen, was wide and long. They'd set a drop-leaf table there and had their family dinners either there or in the solarium at the end of the hall. With a white cloth, candles, and yard holly on the table, it was lovely.

"Are you a surgeon?" Addy asked Sam.

"Passed my Boards last—"

"Then you can carve."

"Is she always so rough-tongued?" Sam complained to Miss Pru.

Tactfully, but with a private, sharp, censuring glance at Addy, Miss Pru replied, "Perhaps she's just worried about Grendel."

"No need," Sam assured her. "Grendel is as healthy as a horse."

"But a very small one." Addy's voice was thin.

"She really is all right." Sam gave Addy a direct serious look of reassurance, and for the first time her eyes clung to his. His lips parted slightly in a soundless gasp, and his expression changed.

Addy's chest was a maelstrom of sensations, and she blurted, "Grendel is illegitimate."

His eyes stayed on hers, and he leaned only an inch toward her as he said in a low voice, "That must have been very, very rough for you."

Addy jerked her head to one side, pulled her napkin onto her lap, and said huskily, "I never would've made it without Miss Pru." Her eyes turned to the older woman. "I owe her our lives."

"Nonsense," Miss Pru denied. "It was Addy who changed my life."

"I had to give up my apartment in Bloomington," Addy explained, "and I moved into Miss Pru's boardinghouse. She sold it to put the down payment on this house. She did the first sewing..."

"Now, now, it wasn't all my doing." Miss Pru turned to Sam. "She began designing and sewing dresses to sell when she was a sophomore in college, so she had a tidy sum saved for herself."

"And when I didn't know what to do about Grendel... and he... had... and my family was still in such shock that they didn't know what to say to me or how to advise me, it was Miss Pru who supported me... in my keeping Grendel... and being practical. Planning. Helping get things done and solved. Miss Pru and then Marcus."

"Marcus?" Sam's voice was intent, his face suddenly still.

"That Marcus." Miss Pru chuckled and clicked her tongue.

Addy's own tongue went on. "Miss Pru found this house. She brought me to look at it, and it was a pile of junk, the boards loose. It was awful."

"The location was excellent," Miss Pru told Sam. "Loose boards could be nailed back and weathered siding could be painted."

"I wanted it white, and Marcus painted it blue," Addy added. "Next he wants to paint it royal blue with lime-green trim, and after that blood-red with mustard trim and—"

"Who's Marcus?" Sam demanded.

Miss Pru and Addy exchanged amused glances. "He lives across the street," Addy told him. "When we moved here, we couldn't figure out a name for the business, and our first blundering choice was the House of Delilah. Everyone knows Delilah was a successful woman, right? Well, the only people who came were some tenacious men who were sure it wasn't really a dress shop. They'd stand on the porch at all hours and swear they weren't the police and all they wanted was a little fun. 'It ain't a raid, baby, honest,'" Addy mimicked in a carefully steadied voice.

"Then we called it Kildaire's," she went on. "But apparently men thought that sounded like a bar, the house standing alone on the block this way. We spent a lot of time arguing through the door in the early morning hours. They'd say, 'Aw, c'mon, honey, open up.' And we'd swear it wasn't a bar and we didn't serve liquor. They'd say, 'Jes' one li'l one? C'mon, Kildaire, we'll drink to Ireland!'

"After that we called it the Gown House." Addy glanced at Sam, but he looked so grim she explained, "The Town House—the Gown House."

"That was very dangerous," he said finally. "The neighborhood in transition and two women alone that way. Anything could have happened."

"Oh, no." Miss Pru waved a dismissive hand. "Marcus always came over and ran them all off."

Addy laughed. "He'd come over the porch rail, looming like a mountain, and say, 'Git!' in that thundering voice of his, and they'd *git!*" She laughed again. "The first time he did that he scared us as much as *them!*"

"Who *is* Marcus?" Sam's voice was tight, and he glared at Addy.

"He's my security," she explained.

With Sam's question supposedly answered, Miss Pru changed the subject. "What exactly does a pediatric consultant do?" Addy was sure Miss Pru knew that answer perfectly well and was just giving him a chance to talk about himself.

Reluctantly Sam turned his attention to Miss Pru. "When a GP or a pediatrician gets stuck, I review the diagnosis and what has been done to see if there's anything that's been ignored or forgotten or if there's anything new or different he or she might try. Therefore I keep up with all the current medical research. I'm rather like a court of last resort."

As he spoke Addy watched him, his manner, his level look, his large, capable hands, and she thought how much the doctors must appreciate his calm, his authority, the fact that he was there to turn to. Baffled, they would find support in him and his knowledge. They would know they'd done the best they could.

"That must be emotionally wearing," Miss Pru said softly. "It must be terribly serious before they come to you."

"All of life is precious, but there are times when it's best to let a child go. Stupidity is the only intolerable thing."

"Jeremy . . . ?" Addy had to ask.

Sam's eyes were steady on her. "He's one of the best." He paused, then asked, "Are you dating Jeremy?"

"Good heavens, no! I've no time for that."

"You don't date at all?" he asked quickly.

"No!" she replied shortly as she began to collect the empty plates.

"Who's Marcus?" he asked yet again as he rose to help her clear the table.

"I told you. He's my security."

"Police or blanket?" he growled.

Addy laughed. "He's married to Hedda, who I think is a female witch doctor. I wouldn't tangle with her under any circumstances, particularly since she caters for us now and then. On top of that, I'm sure he's the Godfather of the Black Mafia."

"Marcus Freeman?" Sam looked very interested.

"Yes, how'd you know?"

"I've heard about him," he said in a thoughtful way, but he didn't elaborate.

They had a trifle for dessert. As Sam licked his lips discreetly, he offered, "I could board here."

"You've been lucky with dinner this time," Addy scoffed.

Miss Pru agreed. "We generally have tea and toast."

"I don't believe that."

"With canned fruits Hedda puts up in the summer," Addy added. "Marcus sells them to us at double the chain-store price." She grinned at him. "Along with being the Godfather, he's also a pirate, so you can see how formidable he is." Now she could handle quick peeks at Sam, but she still couldn't do it calmly. She thought it was smarter not to look at him directly. Even not looking at him, his presence carried an impact that made her too self-conscious, too aware of herself as a woman. Paul had never affected her that way. Sam was so vital and so very attractive, so excessively masculine, that it was just as well he dealt only with children.

After they'd helped Miss Pru clean up the kitchen, they brought another Popsicle up to Grendel. As they climbed the steps, Sam asked, "How's your family now? Concerning Grendel, I mean."

"It was terrible for them," she admitted. "We're from a very small town where the Kildaires have lived forever. Both my parents were very strict, and I shocked them horribly. I had a hard time convincing my father I hadn't been raped or at least forced. My mother was mostly concerned about my two younger sisters. She said it wouldn't have been so bad if it was just me, or if my sisters had been boys, but how could the girls ever say no—and be believed—when everyone knew what their sister had done. Both my parents cried. It was terrible. They love Grendel, but they have problems over her still. I'm sorry about them, but...but I'm so glad I have Grendel."

"Is that why you don't date? You think you're ...ruined?"

"No. I don't want to." She spoke firmly.

"You think your life is over?"

"No, no," she corrected. "I have all I want. I don't have to get involved with another man." She made her mouth prim and lifted her chin, but she didn't look at him.

She felt his eyes on her as he argued with gentle cleverness. "Grendel should be around men enough so that she doesn't get warped." Having planted that thought in her maternal heart, he went ahead of her faltering steps into Grendel's room and began to talk to her cheerfully.

Addy stood in the doorway and listened to their conversation, to the timbre of his deep voice, to how Grendel tried to get her voice down to his level, to how he made her sick child respond.

Addy watched his mouth as he opened it unconsciously as he fed Grendel the mashed Popsicle, how he closed his lips around a nonexistent spoon, and how he licked his lips when Grendel did. She saw how he smiled at her daughter. . . .

Early on Sunday morning Sam came back to see his patient and give Miss Pru a thank-you bouquet for Saturday's dinner. He pretty much ignored Addy, who hung around listening as he explained the button cards he had brought to Grendel which had a big, blunt needle, thick thread for little fingers to control, and buttons with big holes that could be sewn on the cardboard.

In the afternoon he came again and gave Grendel a book that had all sorts of cloth in many textures—velvet to burlap. They identified the different ones together. Grendel, who was her mother's child, could name each and every cloth. She loved the book, but she mourned the missed sledding. She was markedly better, and Sam assured her there would be other times.

When he suggested a trip to the Children's Museum on Wednesday, Addy regretfully said she couldn't, that she had appointments. Sam said that was all right, he hadn't thought she'd be available anyway, but he was counting on taking Grendel. While Grendel whooped and bounced, Addy felt a great wave of disappointment.

Mrs. Harrow, Sam's mother, came for her first fitting on Tuesday and brought a woman with her who had a camera. She was about Sam's age and utterly beautiful. Her name was Diana Hunter, and she was a professional photographer. She asked permission to take some pictures of Grendel, who had recovered fully from her flu by then. Addy gave Diana a distracted go-ahead, assuring her that Grendel would love it because she was a dreadful ham.

At first Addy felt very stiff with Mrs. Harrow, but she relaxed under the older woman's easy manner. Mrs. Harrow had contacted her friends and wanted to confirm a week from Saturday at noon for the showing. Addy said all her models were available and it was all arranged. Mrs. Harrow was very pleased. Addy was even more so.

On Wednesday Addy was in bed with Grendel's flu. She felt rotten and knew she looked worse. Sam came to her door and stood by her bed to tsk. "You're a malingerer," he told her, but he smiled nicely.

Addy was indignant. "I am not! Get out of here!"

But he sat down on the edge of the bed and said, "You look lovely lying there in bed with the covers up to your eyes."

She was hostile and embarrassed. She knew she looked absolutely ghastly. "You'll get the flu."

"Do you have any fever?"

"The way I feel, it's a hundred and ten." She was appalled to hear a self-pitying waver in her voice.

He clicked his tongue once, as if impressed, and said, "That high, huh?"

"Yes."

Then he leaned over and kissed her forehead, and her temperature shot up even higher. "Why did you do that?" she gasped.

"To see if you have a one-hundred-and-ten-degree fever."

"Do I?"

"Almost." He took her hand and held her wrist as he gazed at his watch.

She knew her heart was racing. He'd know, too. She twisted her wrist, trying to wrest it free. He smiled and told her to be still. "It's the three-day flu," she said, "and I don't need a doctor."

He felt the glands under her chin and then down her throat. Then he pulled back the covers and put his head on her chest. "What *are* you doing?" she exclaimed.

"I left my bag in the car, so I don't have my stethoscope with me, and I've got to listen to your heart and how you're breathing."

"And you're doing it that way?"

"Well, of course! How do you think they did it before we had stethoscopes?"

"It was never a problem before. I think you ought to take your head off my chest."

"This is really very nice. I wonder what fool invented the stethoscope?" He sat back up and looked at her, amused.

"You're going to get the flu," she warned him again.

"I'm never sick. It's one of the requirements when you apply for medical school. They have a question on the application, 'Are you ever sick?' If you say no, then you're admitted. If you say yes, you're rejected."

"I can imagine what you put down when they inquired about sex."

He grinned. "What do you think I put down?"

"Either 'yes' or 'often,'" she guessed sardonically.

"I put down 'over.'" He looked down his nose at her.

"That doesn't surprise me. I'm sure you needed the room on the back to fit everything in." She was disapproving.

He ignored her comment and told her she had the three-day flu and didn't need a doctor. She replied stiffly that she'd known that already. He patted her head and told her to stay in bed and be a good girl. She glowered.

Then he took Grendel, who waved from the door, and just left her there. Addy sulked all morning, telling everyone to leave her alone and refusing to drink the mysterious purple stuff Hedda sent over. So Miss Pru and the seamstresses drank the home-canned grape juice instead.

Addy heard Sam and Grendel return in time for Sam to be invited for lunch. Grendel had brought her a pinwheel to put by the hot-air register. When the furnace blower went on, the pinwheel turned madly, its bells ringing. "With all that racket," Sam said, "it will encourage you to get well, if only to get up and make the damned thing be quiet."

Addy gave him a long-suffering glance.

He'd brought her blue Popsicles. He mashed one up and insisted on feeding it to her with a spoon. She sniffled once and said, "I think I'm catching a little cold along with the flu."

He got a cool cloth from the bathroom and wiped her face and gave her almost too much sympathy, then smiled at her and asked, "Do you need to be rocked?"

"Rocked?" she asked incredulously.

He nodded. "Could you wait until after I eat? I'm starved from running after Grendel all morning at the museum, and I need nourishment before I tackle you."

"There's no need for you to 'tackle' me!" Addy stated.

"But I want to!" he protested. "It's what's kept me going all morning."

Just then Miss Pru sent Grendel up to tell Sam lunch was ready, and he had to lean over and kiss Addy's forehead again in order to see if the Popsicle had made her fever go down. But how could it go down when he kept sending it spiraling upward?

It seemed to take two hours for the next thirty minutes to go by. Finally Addy heard Miss Pru and Grendel in the hall. She was propped up on an elbow, straining to hear Sam's voice, when the door opened and he walked in.

"You didn't knock," she accused him, embarrassed.

"Doctors never knock. It's one of the perks."

She pulled the covers back up to her nose and lay back down. He sat down beside her, his face kind, his smile amused, as usual. She asked politely, "Did you have a nice time? Did Grendel behave?" It was awkward to make conversation with a man who was sitting on the side of the bed, especially such an attractive man. Drawing-room conversation seemed inappropriate under the circumstances.

"She was perfect," Sam said. "She's been raised well."

The words "I wondered..." were torn from Addy, but she stopped, and her fingers played with the top of the quilt.

As if he could read her mind, he said, "I had something else in mind for you."

Her eyes flew to him. "What?" she asked, as if she hadn't really heard him.

"There's a Bluegrass concert Saturday. Do you like that kind of music?"

"I love it," she said without thinking.

"Will you go ... with me?"

"Oh, yes," she said, so quickly that she didn't think

what she was saying. Then she qualified it with "Well . . . if I'm healthy enough," which left it open so that she could beg off later.

But he said casually, "You're already committed."

The concert began rollicking and ended sentimental, and the whole performance was very satisfying. Addy had worn a red, scoop-necked, long-sleeved wool dress with a black velvet cape, and she looked terrific. He'd told her that. Her high-heeled short boots were black velvet with red lining as was her muff. He said she was good advertising for her Gown House, that all the women were jealous of her and wondering where she'd found such a smashing outfit.

Addy blushed with pleasure, but she didn't say what she was thinking, that he was partly right—the women were envious of her, but only because he was her escort.

When he took her home, he walked to the door with her and kissed her good night. It shattered her. She behaved disgracefully. She kissed him back and gasped and clung to his shoulders, and her blood turned to molten fire as sensual thrills surged through her body. To be kissed by him . . . to be held . . . to feel his lips on hers and on her face. To be held to him, close to his body! She dropped her muff and didn't even realize she had until he stooped and handed it back to her.

He smiled down at her, his eyes seeming to spark with fire as he leaned over to give her a gentle kiss on the cheek. Then he opened the door and helped her over the threshold and said good night.

She wasn't capable of replying. She stood in the open doorway, letting all the heat out of the house as she watched him walk to his car and drive away.

His kisses had been so different from Paul's. Paul's had never made her feel this way. Her whole body was in an uproar—and wanting more! She'd never had such kisses.

Obviously she was experiencing a sexual response to Sam's kisses. This was what the biology books talked about and what romances proclaimed as being worth all the trouble. She groaned as desire licked through her body at the thought of Sam's kisses. It was a strange kind of agony, but not unpleasant.

Addy's legs were getting cold, so she finally closed the door, wandered up to her room, undressed, and crawled into bed all in a trance. But she wasn't so far gone that she didn't hear the furnace laboring to replace the lost heat.

The next day she'd regained control. When Sam called, she replied in a casual way that should have put him off a little. "I enjoyed the concert," he said, "but I enjoyed our good-night better."

Deliberately pretending he meant his leaving her, she replied, "I realized you must be tired. I too had an early night." He laughed. Only then did she remember it had been almost one o'clock when they'd parted, which didn't qualify as an early night. Calling it that revealed how short the evening in his company had seemed to her.

The three young women who had accompanied Sam and his mother to the special showing came at various times for their fittings. Addy felt sure they were Sam's mistresses, because none was named Mrs. Samuel Grady. Later she learned they were his half-sister and two step-sisters, whereupon her attitude toward them changed remarkably.

A week after Diana Hunter had taken the pictures of Grendel, she returned with the prints and showed them to Addy. At first Addy thought Diana was selling her the prints, but gradually she realized Diana was talking about hiring Grendel as a photographer's model. "Grendel?" Addy asked, surprised.

"She's a natural model. She can look any way I suggest! Just look at these!" Diana gestured to the variety of expressions shown in the scattered pictures.

"Well, she is a ham...."

"How about it? We pay standard fees, and she could save up the money for college." When Addy still hesitated, Diana asked, "What's the trouble?"

"I'm afraid she might turn into a smug little mirror-conscious prig," Addy admitted.

"Not Grendel. She thinks it's fun. Like acting stories. We'll be quick enough, and treat her ordinarily enough so that she won't feel so special. I promise."

"Well, we could give it a try, and if we see signs of her being spoiled, we could stop," Addy said, relenting.

"Good enough. I'll pick her up and deliver her home. And, Addy, we'll be careful of her. I promise that too."

"She's so young and little."

Diana laughed. "She's a sturdy little tease. She's a survivor."

Thinking of all they'd survived so far, Addy agreed.

CHAPTER FIVE

THE FIRST PICTURE of Grendel appeared in the *Journal*, and Addy received some nice compliments from people who saw it. The toy advertisement didn't mention Grendel's name but, later in the month, after her picture was used again, there was an article on photographer's models, and a picture of Grendel was included as someone new to the field. It said her name was Grendel Kildaire and her mother was a designer of women's clothes.

Grendel modeled four times that month for an hour each time. Diana treated her in a businesslike way. She set up lights and backgrounds ahead of time and took the pictures rapidly while Grendel acted out a story. Grendel loved it, and Addy was a little shocked by how much a three-year-old could earn in four hours.

On the day of the showing Addy arranged for Mrs. Harrow, Sam arrived with his mother's group. He was the only man in the room. Most other men would have felt ill at ease, Addy thought, but not Sam. He sat in the front row, and when she came out onto the platform in a two-piece wool tartan, he winked at her.

After that she went into some sort of time warp. Her eyes retained the image of Sam and, although she sat on the stool and her eyes were directed toward the models and her mouth gave out her memorized narration, her real self contemplated Sam's image clearly imprinted in her mind. She mused over it. That mouth had kissed hers. Those arms had held her close. Those eyes had smiled down into hers. She'd been pressed against that body.

In her bemused haze she watched as her daughter danced out onto the runway. Grendel put her chin on her chest and pulled her mouth down in concentration as she showed the ladies—and one man—that she could undo her own buttons. All of her clothes fastened in front with buttons that were big enough for her tiny hands to handle. Grendel's modeling sold a lot of children's clothes.

Of course, that day Addy didn't model. She wasn't about to get up in front of Sam's mother on a runway. Not that she was interested in Sam, or that he was interested in her, or anything like that, so it didn't matter what Elizabeth Turner Harrow thought one way or the other. But, Addy decided, there are times you did things and times when you'd rather not, and modeling for Mrs. Harrow and her friends that day was one time she'd rather not.

Even in her daze she considered her attitude silly. Her business was clothes, the showing and selling of them, and she suspected for some strange reason that she was being pretty dumb. She should straighten up and behave and not let some devastating man, whom she had no use for at all, interfere in her business life.

As she straightened up on the stool, she knew his eyes were riveted on her, watching every move. Good grief! How perfectly ridiculous. It was just like her to be paranoid that way. Why would he look at her? She continued listening absently to herself speaking, then carefully turned her head a bare notch and, glancing as far to the right as she could, peeked at Sam. He *was* watching her!

She'd been right. She wasn't paranoid after all. Her heart thundered, her palms grew moist, her breath caught, and she had to swallow in the middle of a word, though her mouth was so dry she had nothing to swallow, and it sounded awful. Her tongue darted out and licked her lips, and then things went more smoothly.

At last the whole ordeal was over. The ladies had loved it. Addy could hear the one man's heavier clapping and his low voice amidst the twittering of the women. She felt she'd run the mile in less than four minutes in high heels.

Hedda had arranged cakes in the parlor, and Miss Pru poured the tea and served the dainty food. The ladies milled around, calling cheerfully to one another, exclaiming over materials and ordering copies for themselves. They weren't in any hurry to leave. It was a real party.

Sam eased up to Addy and said, "I came specifically to see you model the robe again." He chewed his lower lip, and his eyes spilled laughter as he watched her blush.

"You bought the robe and another one hasn't been made up yet," she replied rather tartly.

"Make it red," he suggested.

She frowned. "Red?"

"Men like red."

"I'm not selling to men."

"You sold me." Had he said it that way deliberately?

"Did she . . . like the . . . robe?" Addy forced out the question despite her agony. Whom had he given it to?

"I haven't given it to her yet."

"Oh." She looked off sadly, then had to ask, "Why didn't you let us clean it?"

"I'll take care of that," he assured her. In a whisper he added, "I can smell your perfume in it."

The most erotic thrill flooded her as she imagined him holding the robe to his face and breathing of it deeply, inhaling the scent of her. She imagined him allowing the robe to slide down his naked body as he inhaled the essence of her. Good lord!

She pursed her lips and straightened her backbone and asked primly, "Would you like some cake?" He said he wasn't quite through with the one he had. She looked stupidly at his hands and wondered how the plate and fork had so magically flown into them.

She excused herself formally and went to the kitchen and held a tea towel under the cold faucet until it was soaked and her hand was turning numb from the cold. Then she squeezed the excess water from the towel and put it to her face in gentle pats so as not to disturb her makeup.

Hedda leaned around her and frowned questioningly into her face. Addy wondered if Hedda really couldn't speak or if she just didn't bother to. "Yes. Headache," Addy told her.

Hedda reached into a voluminous pocket in her long purple skirt and took out two black pills. She handed them to Addy, who took one look at them and knew they were voodoo. The black of the pills was probably dried chicken blood. It was African witch medicine. She peeked cautiously at Hedda. Her expression was serene. It would be. She hadn't had two strange pills thrust at her with an enigmatic, watchful face seeing if she had the courage to swallow them.

Addy looked at the pills in her palm with a good deal of anxiety, but at last she popped them into her mouth. Hedda stopped her abruptly and frowned furiously, then chewed elaborately. Addy chewed obediently. They were after-dinner mints soaked in licorice. So much for voo-doo.

Having swallowed the mints, Addy stood leaning against the sink, looking out the window at the winter-scape and thinking that a psychological remedy for a psychological headache made sense. Maybe her imagination was getting out of hand. Sam was just a man, a man made up of muscle and bone and hair. But it was all arranged in such a maddeningly attractive manner.

She wondered what God had been up to to make a man like Sam. It really wasn't fair. Sam ought not to be allowed out among ordinary mortal females. Any sane woman wanted the best of men, and Sam was the best. So did she want him? How impossible! She shook her-self, put down the glass, and gently burped licorice. Come to think of it, she didn't much like licorice. She frowned at Hedda, who gave her a black look and then ignored her.

Addy went back to the milling, chatting women and stood around being polite and pretending not to know exactly where Sam was the whole time. Almost half the women there were his age. Addy had him figured for being somewhere in his late thirties. She watched not Sam but all the young women who talked to him easily and in a friendly manner. He replied to them in kind. And not wanting him and with no chance of having him, Addy was jealous.

As he was leaving, Sam found time for a minute with

her and said, "Would you come out with me tomorrow
with Miss Pru and Grendel? We could go to brunch at
the Marten House."

She nodded. Even knowing she was foolish and had
no business walking on the railroad track and pretending
she could avoid being hit by the train, she nodded. One
more time would be all right. That was what she told
herself. One more time.

Several days later, when Sam suggested they go see
a play, that was what Addy told herself again—one more
time wouldn't hurt. But she looked over her entire ward-
robe and found nothing right or pretty or suitable. So
she dropped everything else and sketched a gown, se-
lected the material, and, ignoring the knowing glances of
her staff, appropriated Emmaline's machine and sewed
it herself. The material was velvet—and it was red. She
wasn't dumb. He'd said men liked red.

The gown had long, straight, slightly flared sleeves,
with wide filigreed braids at the wrists, which were hell
to sew. The neck was square, and that too was bordered
in the braid. Addy didn't know one single client she'd
have done all that work for, but she did it for herself,
humming contentedly. The dress was fitted and the skirt
was long. She wore a pink velvet coat with a fur-trimmed
hood and a fur muff. She had pink, high-heeled ankle
boots. Her lipstick matched the red dress exactly.

She knew the play was funny because everyone burst
out laughing and exchanged amused glances with the
people next to them. She smiled with the laughter, staring
at the stage, conscious only of the man to her right.

During intermission the laughter continued, and the
buzz of talk was animated and noisy. Sam got them
glasses of wine and, as they stood sipping, Addy said,
"It's funny."

Sam grinned. "I haven't been paying much attention.

You're so gorgeous I can't concentrate on anything else."

"Addy!" a male voice interrupted.

She turned blank eyes and saw a nice-looking young man she hadn't seen in several years. "Oh, hello, Jim." She introduced the two men.

Jim was perfunctory in his response to Sam and kept his eyes on Addy. "How great to see you! So you're dating now?"

What could she say? There she was, all dressed up and obviously with a date. She nodded reluctantly and said lamely, "A little."

Jim grinned and said, "Good! I'll call you." Then, ignoring Sam altogether, he touched Addy's shoulder in an intimate gesture and walked away.

There was a pause, then Sam said, "Who was that?" in a carefully neutral tone.

"Jim Hardy."

"I see. And what business does he have ogling you that way?"

"He didn't." She shrugged.

"You couldn't see the way he was eyeing you?"

She shook her head. Why was he questioning her this way? He had no right at all. He bought women robes with *hooks* on them and now he was hostile over an old friend for saying hello to her. He had a lot of nerve.

When the play was over, they were silent among the chattering crowd as they left the theater and walked to Sam's car. They drove through the cold streets before he spoke. "If that guy calls for a date, tell him you have one. Then call me and you will. I don't like the look of him at all."

"Oh, Sam, that's not—"

"Yes, it is. Do you understand? Just tell me when."

She sighed in exasperation as she watched the road. The houses were dark, only the yellow streetlights shining on the snow. He turned into the driveway of the unlit Gown House and brought the car to a stop. When she started to get out, he touched her arm. When she looked around to see why, he kissed her.

She made it easy for him. He pushed back her hood and undid the two buttons at the neckline and opened the coat so that he could put his arms around her velvet-clad body and pull her close to him, then closer as his kiss deepened.

Her heart pounded and her blood surged, roaring in her ears. All this couldn't be very good for her body. Getting all excited like that had to affect her blood pressure. She'd probably have a heart attack. But she didn't stop kissing him back, distracted by the wondrous sensual writhings licking inside her body. It would be worth a heart attack to feel that way. Why hadn't Paul's kisses ever done this to her?

Even with her mind soaked in erotic sensations, the thought of Paul caused her to get hold of herself. She might not have been particularly interested in having sex with Paul, but she was definitely interested in a much closer encounter with Sam. That really shocked her, because she *knew* what it was like, and it hadn't been much fun.

But there was no way in the world she was going to get caught in that trap again. She tried to turn her mouth away from Sam's, but his just followed hers. She took her hands from his hair and tried to wedge them between their bodies, but there wasn't any room. When she wriggled, he just purred.

Finally, when he turned his attention to her throat, she managed to gasp, "I've got to go in now." She'd meant to say, "Stop it this minute!" but it came out "I've got to go in now." Then she could have bitten her damned tongue, for he paused. She hadn't meant him to obey quite so fast. In fact, he could have ignored her for another minute or two, couldn't he?

He appeared reluctant to release her as he slowly lifted his head and loosened his arms. He stroked his hands over the soft velvet, not speaking, then said, "It's been a great evening. Thank you."

"No, thank *you*. I enjoyed the play. It was so funny."

"What was?"

"The play." How could she tell what had been funny about it when she hadn't paid attention to it?

"What did you like best?"

"Oh..." She searched furiously for some fragment of the play for a clue and finished lamely, "The whole thing."

He apparently accepted that. "Remember, if that guy calls you, you're busy."

"He won't."

"Yes, he will. I know that look."

"What look?"

"The way he ogled you."

"That's silly." She opened the door and swung her dainty pink boots into the snow.

"Quit rushing," Sam growled as he put a staying hand on her arm. Then he swung open his own door, slid out of the car, and came around to her side, offering her his hand. As she headed toward the porch, he stopped her and gestured with one gloveless hand at the woods. "It's beautiful."

She gazed at the still, moonlit tangle of black limbs against the snow. She parted her lips to remark on how it looked like lace, but he bent his head and kissed her again. They clung together in the snow and freezing cold, warmed by their heated blood.

Eventually Sam released her, and she found herself inside the house, watching him drive away. She stood in the entrance hall, lit by an Edison lamp, and contemplated her passion-racked body. The train was coming closer.

With so many of Mrs. Harrow's friends ordering copies of her summer line, Addy had to add two more seamstresses to her regular staff. She again told Marcus that Emmaline was not pulling her weight, and it was a good thing she only paid her by the piece, because she'd go broke supporting Emmaline on hourly wages. Marcus said not to fret, that Emmaline would work out.

Addy waved her arms around. "Two other women could use Emmaline's machine and never interrupt her."

"How's her work?" Marcus asked, unmoved.

In exasperation, Addy admitted, "Beautiful."

"Well? Then why are you fussing?"

"Oh, Marcus, she puts too much time into everything. It's *too* perfect. Her seams will be perfect after the material has rotted away! They'll still be perfect in a thousand years when they dig up central Indiana!"

"Addy," Marcus scolded patiently, "you do tend to get a little hyper. Give her time . . ."

"That's her problem! She takes too much time. She drifts around as if she's on another planet and not quite in touch with this one."

"Be patient."

"I'll be patient all right. A mental patient!"

To protect herself from Sam, Addy stopped answering the phone. She heard the train whistle every time his name was spoken. But it didn't particularly surprise her one day when she and Grendel were at the Children's Museum and who should come along with a great smile to lift a squealing, welcoming Grendel up above his head but—of course—Sam.

Addy tagged along, watching as the large man and

the fairy child explored and exclaimed over the general
store and the farmyard, and rode the merry-go-round.
The rapport between them was so obvious that one middle-aged woman, standing next to Addy and watching
them, said, "You can sure tell who her daddy is." She
laughed comfortably and added, "There's no blaming
that one on the milkman."

Addy slid a horrified glance to Sam, who was beaming
a smug grin at the woman, taking full credit for Grendel!
Addy's tongue stumbled over the words as she said, "He
isn't my husband."

The woman's smile faded. "Oh? Well. There's a lot
of you girls keeping the kid now." Solemnly she nodded
in agreement with her words as the trio remained silent,
then added with a smile, "At least you're friends, and
the little one will know her daddy. That's smart of you."
She turned to Sam. "Are you married to someone else?"

Instead of explaining, he replied simply, "No."

"Well." She eyed Grendel. "With a little gem like
that, you ought to think about fixing things up between
you. You look like a nice little family. And she shouldn't
be an only child."

Addy stuttered, "Well, you know . . . he's not . . . and
I'm . . . she . . ."

Sam just looked at Addy with concentrated interest,
and the woman patted her shoulder and said, "I know,
but learn to cook and don't hop into bed with him again
until he makes it legal."

Addy could only gasp, "I can already cook!"

Leaving them, the woman told Addy, "Don't . . . do
the other. Got it?" And with a conspiratorial wink, she
was gone.

During the rest of the afternoon Sam was filled with
laughter. Every time he caught Addy's eyes, his were
spilling over with humor. "Good lord, Sam," she said,

"why didn't you tell her?" And she said, "Oh, quit that!" and she huffed, "You think this is all a big joke!" Then she ended up glaring into his laughing eyes, not saying, but thinking, Oh, Sam, you're so gorgeous. I wish you *were* Grendel's father. I wish it had been you.

But as they were leaving they saw the woman again. She gave them a knowing glance, and Sam said to Grendel, "Come along, honey, Mommy's waiting." And it sounded...it sounded as if...The woman gave Addy an encouraging nod and a cautioning shake of her finger.

CHAPTER SIX

ALTHOUGH MISS PRU denied it, Addy decided Sam must be in close contact with her, because Addy kept running into him every time she went someplace, and he couldn't possibly have time to spend spying on her to find out where she was going. Her stupid heart was exhausted from going from normal into a thundering high at the sight of him. Her lungs were tired of panting, and her body was going into a decline from longing. She wasn't eating well, and she was a little vague. Her designs turned dreamy and romantic, with ruffles and lace and soft materials.

Miss Pru sent her to match some thread, and there in the fabric shop was Sam! He said hello as if astonished to find her there. She eyed him suspiciously. "Did Miss Pru call you?"

"Does she need me?" he asked.

"What are you doing here?"

"I'm matching some thread for Mother." He picked up some black thread. "Why else would I be here?" His expression was serious, but there was a betraying sparkle in his eyes.

"Why didn't she get it herself?"

"Oh, you know Mother. She's at another meeting and didn't have the time."

"But you did?" Addy mocked.

"Hey, it's a good thing I ran into you. I have an extra ticket to the hockey game. You can have it."

"You're not going to use it?" Occasionally people gave her tickets and she passed them on to Marcus, who found someone to go to the event.

"Nope. Here." He took the ticket from his breast pocket and started to hand it to her, then looked at it again and took it back, saying, "That one's mine."

Then he reached into his pocket again and said, "This one's yours." But instead of giving it to her, he just said, "I'll pick you up at six, and we'll just have hamburgers first so you'll have room for hot dogs later during the game." He leaned over and kissed her cheek and walked out—to the blast of train whistles coming closer.

Several nights later, feeling as if her body was being rushed helplessly into a sort of Armageddon over which she had no control, Addy found herself sitting about ten rows off the ice watching a bloodthirsty hockey game.

It was astonishing to her how the crowd was filled with bloodlust. They made no pretense of practicing good sportsmanship or of being fair-minded. They yelled and booed and cheered and shouted, vitally involved with every play. In Roman times they'd have been for the lions.

It was all very noisy and exhausting, but mostly Addy was waiting to go home. It wasn't that she was bored or not feeling well or anything like that. It was that when he took her home he would probably kiss her again. She sat there, her eyes obediently following the play while she thought about Sam kissing her. The excitement of anticipation licked her stomach.

He often looked at her and smiled, jammed next to her in his seat, their shoulders rubbing, his thigh alongside hers, shifting and touching. Her body reacted to his. When everyone leaped to their feet and she responded automatically to the move, he put his arm around her shoulders or his hand on her waist. His touch filled her with shivers of sensual pleasure, and the game was wasted on her. She was conscious only of Sam.

He brought her hot dogs and watched her eat them. He licked his own lips as she licked hers. And he laughed down at her and appeared to relish the game and being there. When they left in the closely packed, slowly moving crowd, he went first, holding her hand securely behind him and keeping her close as he made a protected pathway for her.

Outside, as they walked to his car, their breaths frosted in the air. Addy shivered in the cold car as they waited for the traffic to ease so they could pull out into the stream of traffic.

"The heater will warm up in a minute." Sam grinned down at her. "Would you like to go to a dirty, crowded, noisy, smoky old bar? Or should we go to your house and make some hot cocoa?"

What could she say to that? That she wanted to go to a crowded, dirty old bar? She couldn't hide a grin as she said, "The cocoa." When he laughed, it was so intimate that anticipation wriggled inside her. If he came inside, he'd be rude not to kiss her. Or she could kiss him—

casually, of course—as she told him she'd enjoyed the evening. It would be just a light, friendly kiss, nothing steamy or sexual or anything like that, just a pleasant, casual kiss. Preoccupied by her thoughts, she was startled at how quickly they arrived at her house.

She unlocked the door and, after they'd moved inside, she closed it carefully. The house was so big that any sound seemed to reverberate. Feeling awkward in the entrance hall alone with Sam, Addy called his attention to the red crystal lamp that hung in the stairwell. It was Art Nouveau, swirled in silver, and had an original light bulb from Edison's day that still burned.

"It's occasionally mentioned in the *Journal* as an interesting item, and now and then someone comes by and asks to look at it."

Sam looked up obediently and said, "Ummm."

"There are sealed bets as to how much longer it'll last," she told Sam in hushed tones.

"What do you bet?" He took off his coat.

"I don't know." She hung it with hers in the cavernous closet under the stair landing. As she emerged from the depths, closed the door, and turned, he took her into his arms and kissed her. She melted against him. Her first thought was how nice that he'd done it right away without making her wait until he was leaving.

After that, sensation took over, and she simply leaned against him and allowed her body to absorb all the waves of marvelous thrills his kiss produced in her. She was disappointed when he finally lifted his mouth and looked down into her face. Feeling bereft, although still locked in his arms, she made a discontented sound and lifted her mouth as if seeking his.

His pleased chuckle made her eyes pop open as she realized what she'd done. She swallowed and pushed against him until he slowly released her. He allowed her to leave his arms. She wasn't sure why she'd insisted, so she smoothed her hair and tugged her clothes into place. She shot a glance at him and saw him watching her with an amused smile. Why did he think she was funny? Was he laughing at her? She supposed she *had* fallen very quickly into his arms and returned his kisses in a very unladylike manner.

She turned blindly and groped in the darkness beyond the lighted entrance hall. She blundered into a table, then into the wall, her attention on Sam as he followed her. He took her arm and led her. She babbled in a whisper, "You must eat your carrots, you see so well in the dark."

He said he was part cat. She said, "Oh," as if that explained everything, thinking about panthers who were blue-eyed and beautiful and fascinating even if rather frightening.

In the kitchen Addy switched on the light and closed the door to the back hall. Then she opened a cupboard, and three pans slid out onto the floor with loud clangs. She froze, listening, then gasped, "Miss Pru will think there are burglars."

"Why do you call her Miss Pru?"

"I couldn't call her Prudence, and she's such a lady that I had to call her something with a title. But Miss Walker sounded so formal with all we'd gone through together. So I settled on Miss Pru. Now everyone calls her that."

"Miss Walker?" Sam asked.

"She never married. I believe there was a tragedy back during World War Two. I've never had the courage to ask." She removed the lid from the cake dish. "Hedda left some lemon tea cakes here. Would you like some?"

"Sounds good," he agreed. "Are we going to eat in here? I could set the table."

"There's a little parlor in the front of the house. It

was always kept exclusively for company in the olden days. Since we use the drawing room as a reception or showroom, we keep the little parlor for visitors. There's a fireplace. Would you like to go in there?"

"Umm-hmm." He smiled.

She led him from the kitchen to the parlor through the dining room. She turned on lamps so that he could light the firewood while she went back to the kitchen. There she got out a silver chocolate pot and a silver bowl for marshmallows. First she filled the pot with hot milk and set it aside to warm so that it wouldn't chill the cocoa later. Then she lay a lace doily on a plate before lifting the tiny lemon cakes onto it. She put forks and spoons and linen napkins on the tray. She emptied the milk from the chocolate pot, poured in the cocoa, and put that on the tray too.

Sam came back to the kitchen just then, his jacket off, his shirt-sleeves turned up, and his collar unbuttoned. He looked as if he planned to stay awhile. Addy sneaked a cautious eye at the clock. It was only a bit after eleven. She promised herself to be careful and not let things get out of hand. That is, she would stay out of Sam's hands.

Sam's smile was self-satisfied, but there were no canary feathers clinging to that panther's mouth... yet. Resolute, she nodded when he asked if the tray was ready and went ahead of him into the parlor. Step into my parlor, said the spider to the fly. Was she the spider or the fly? The fire was going nicely, but what caught her eye was that Sam had moved a small sofa and a marble-topped occasional table in front of it. The sofa only seated two people. Addy sat gingerly on the edge of "her" sofa pillow, clasping her hands, her knees—and her lips— tightly pressed together.

With fluid ease, Sam sat down on "his" sofa pillow and sprawled over onto hers, his muscular thigh against her hip. Sensations burst through her from his touch. All that just from the touch of his thigh against her hip! She probably should plead a headache and go to bed.

He'd probably agree, go with her, and examine her— *sans* thermometer and stethoscope—and then he'd probably decide she needed an injection. She'd better settle down and get control of herself. She turned to him. "Marshmallows?" she asked politely, thinking that was what she was with him, a helpless marshmallow.

"There's no other way," he began seriously.

Her head floated. Her eyes met his and her mouth parted. No other way? Did he mean . . . ? "W-what?"

"The only way to drink cocoa is with marshmallows," he said reasonably.

"Oh." Her head jerked up, but she brought it down slowly. As her eyes came down level with his again, she noted that he was watching her quizzically, with the same amused gleam in his eyes.

Reminding herself how much trouble one brief encounter with a man had once been for her, she schooled herself to regain control, poured the cocoa, added the marshmallows, and remained sitting forward on the edge of the sofa.

Why was she such a shambles and he so calm? They always said men were the ones who were avidly sexual and women aloof. What was wrong with her? She had never been this way with Paul. The only reason she'd acquiesced to Paul at all was that he'd been so upset . . . and anyway, everyone else she knew was either sleeping with someone or living with someone.

It had been embarrassing with Paul, and she hadn't liked it at all. She'd been so disappointed that she'd cried. He'd said all virgins did that, and he'd gone to sleep, leaving her to wonder if she was weird. Other women liked it. They said so. Had they lied?

"You're awfully quiet." Sam's voice was intimately low and husky.

She gave him a quick, prim smile and sipped her cocoa. She found herself wondering if . . . it . . . would be different with Sam. She blushed and lifted a piece of lemon cake to take a bite, but decided her mouth was too dry, she wouldn't be able to chew or swallow it and she'd choke, and he'd pat her on the back and be darling to her and . . . She put the cake down on the tray.

"Not hungry after all?" he asked.

"Uh . . . well . . . we had a big dinner . . ."

"We just had hamburgers and later hot dogs," he reminded her.

"Well . . . I had a snack this afternoon. With Grendel. She's modeling for Diana Hunter. Isn't it marvelous that her family named her Diana . . . you know, having Hunter for a last name, and Diana is the goddess of the hunt and all? She's a professional photographer." Addy ignored the fact that he was nodding agreement at her every word. "And Grendel thinks it's such fun. . . ." She wound down and then stopped completely.

"Mother told Diana about Grendel. She's an old friend."

"Oh?" Addy looked at him, her jaw falling.

"Of the family," he explained. "Her mother and mine were sorority sisters."

"Yes, I see." And of course, she did see. That's how Mrs. Harrow contrived to matchmake. "I'll just bring Diana over with me. Will Sam be there?" Addy *had* liked Diana. How tricky of her to be likable.

"Hurry up and finish that damned cocoa," he growled at her.

Naturally he would growl, being a panther. He wanted her to lean back so he could . . . lick her feathers off . . . and then he'd purr. She would like to make him purr. Why, Adelina Mary Rose Kildaire! she exclaimed to herself. No wonder you were an unmarried mother! Then she argued back to herself: Only one man and it was hardly depraved behavior. Then she concluded: it's all mental, and he'll never know how he affects me.

"What in the world are you thinking?" Sam asked. "Your lips are working, your head is making tiny movements, and your breathing is fast, as if you're arguing with ghosts."

She turned again to look at him. He was lying back with relaxed grace, the firelight playing over his marvelous face and body. She thought of his words, "arguing with ghosts," and said, "You're not far from the mark."

"Tell me," he invited.

But she shook her head and turned her face pensively to the firelight. If she'd been slated to make a big mistake, as she had once in her life, why couldn't she have waited and made it with Sam?

"Is this old house haunted?" he asked unexpectedly.

"Once a woman came here to buy a dress and said this was a very busy house. I thought she meant our business and smiled at her, but she said spirits roamed here."

"Do you believe that?"

She shrugged. "If there are spirits, they're friendly."

"Why did you decide to keep Grendel after she was born?"

"Perhaps I'm basically selfish." She was looking into the fire. "I sought out all the advice, and the professional people were amazingly kind and didn't burden me with guilt. Their attitude was to allow the past to be past and learn from it. They all gave good, solid information on the pros and cons of keeping her or giving her up. They leaned toward giving her up. But then when she was born, I couldn't.

"Miss Pru just listened to me. She'd been tnere all along, and she never once said what she really thought. My family was still shattered. Talking to them was such an ordeal for them that it was kinder to leave them alone. They were even torn over whether or not I should keep her.

"It might have helped if she hadn't looked like Paul, but she's very different from our family. We're all blond and blue-eyed. In our town, when they talk about a certain redheaded child, their eyes are knowing, as if they think his mother was unfaithful. She was one of our family, so she escaped being shunned. If she'd been an outsider, her life would've been hell. Then an old cousin of my grandmother's came to visit and saw the child and said, 'So the red strain finally popped up again. It's been so long we thought it was lost.' And she traced it back two hundred years.

"Paul, being of French descent, with his olive complexion and brown eyes, was truly foreign to them. They met him once."

"Has he ever seen Grendel?"

"I haven't heard from him since I told him I was pregnant. He turned and walked out of the apartment and never came back. He doesn't know if I kept the baby or if I lost it, or if it was a boy or girl, whole or afflicted. Nothing. One big zero."

"That hurts." Sam's low voice was very kind.

"I hadn't wanted the relationship. I had my life planned, and marriage was far in the future. I'd been strictly raised, but it seemed to me that everyone had a relationship going and *that* was normal and I wasn't. It wasn't peer pressure. No one cared what I did or didn't do.

"He said he loved me madly and couldn't survive without me, that he'd die if I didn't sleep with him. And he did look awful—thin, eyes sunken, nervous. I felt sorry for him."

"So you moved in with him."

"No. He lived in a dorm. I had an apartment, and he just didn't leave one night. I couldn't throw him out, and we argued until I was exhausted. Then he...It was awful."

Sam rubbed the back of her neck in a soothing way, massaging the tense muscles. His long fingers were strong and gentle, and Addy began to relax. After a while he observed, "You've never forgiven yourself, have you?"

She didn't reply for a while. Then she said in a very low voice, "I broke the rules."

"And rules are important because they save a lot of trouble and grief. That goes for traffic rules, health rules, or sex. But having been in a wreck doesn't mean you have to agonize over it for the rest of your life."

"There's Grendel," Addy reminded him.

"She's a darling little girl."

"Oh, I'm not sorry I have her, but what about her? Will she hate me when she's old enough to know all about it?"

"You could have had an abortion," he told her, "but you didn't."

"No." She'd never considered it.

"There will be people who disapprove of everything you did. They won't change. And we need people who value rules, for they don't allow the conduct of civilization to become too lax. But there will be those who can adjust and accept you for the caring woman you are. They'll recognize your struggle and understand it. You didn't keep Grendel as a whim or plaything or a doll substitute. You aren't on welfare or making the government support you. You're self-sustaining and you've made it."

"Miss Pru was essential. I couldn't have done it without her."

"Yes, you could have. You're very strong."

"I don't feel that way."

"You're invincible. You might worry and fret, but you'd make it." And she knew he was right.

They were quiet for a while, watching the fire, listening to it crackle. "So the spirits in the house are friendly?" Sam asked.

Addy replied, "Yes," but she was distracted. Her whole body was responding to Sam's long fingers working lazy circles on her shoulders.

"I'm a friendly spirit too," he said. Then he tugged her body back and turned her expertly so that she was pressed against him.

Her eyes almost pleaded with him. For what? Did she want to be taken or released? She didn't know. He arranged her comfortably, taking his time, touching her lingeringly, until she was nestled just right. He lifted her hands to the back of his head and ran his own up her arms and across her shoulders as his hot eyes examined her eyes, her face, her mouth. And then he kissed her.

His hands moved on her, down her back, to her hips, up again to cradle her head against the pressure of his kiss; as the kiss softened and opened, his hand moved to her waist and up to press the softness of the side of her breast. He shifted his body, released her mouth, and planted kisses along her throat, the pressure of his mouth nudging her head back over his arm, exposing more of her throat. Then he turned her just a little to allow his hand to cup her breast.

Her body reacted to his stroking, touching, and to his

kissing. The surface of her skin became excited, and waves of sensations skittered over her. Deeper, sensual curls of awareness licked up through her body to her brain and sent her blood reeling. Her hands closed around his head, and she pressed him closer, and the secret places of her body tingled and shivered.

When she made no protest, his hands and mouth became more urgent. His lips sought hers again. His tongue began a gentle intrusion, flicking, touching, seeking. She groaned and sighed and lay pliant in his arms.

"I want you." His voice shook, and his breathing was erratic.

"I know." She lay there as if helpless.

"Make love with me," he urged.

"No." She could barely make her languid lips form the word.

"No?" He seemed to have a little trouble realizing what she'd said.

"I don't dare," she replied with a sad sigh.

"Addy, I have protection."

But instead of his words comforting her or reassuring her, her eyes popped open and she looked at him, offended. "Oh, you do!" She sat up, turned, and perched huffily on the edge of her sofa pillow, straightening her hair and blouse.

"Hey!" he protested in a soft voice, looking confused.

"So you carry protection around just in case . . ."

"That's not true."

"Oh, no? Then why do you have it with you? You thought that just because Grendel's illegitimate, I'd be a pushover!"

"Now, Addy . . ."

"Well, I'm not! I've learned my lesson *very* well! And just because—"

"You're paranoid about Grendel! You think you have

illegitimate child' written all over you—and backwards on your forehead so it can be read in the rearview mirror!"

"No. But you just want me to let you sleep with me . . ."

"Okay. I'm willing!" He was very irritated.

"Well, I won't!"

"You weren't objecting all this time." She resented his pointing that out.

There was a short silence. Then she bowed her head, and said in a thin voice, "I know. I'm sorry. But it wasn't like anything I'd ever . . ." She fell silent.

But his ears had caught that, and he perked up considerably as he urged, "It wasn't?" She shook her head and kept her face turned away. "Addy, look at me." He put his arm around her stiff body, while his other hand turned her face slowly to him. But she kept her eyes down. "Addy, when I saw you on the runway, showing that robe, you knocked me sideways. Every time I've seen you, you've made my head spin a little more. I brought along protection tonight in case you invited me to spend the night. When I've touched you, you haven't seemed disgusted."

"You thought I'd . . ." She looked up indignantly.

"I'd rather have it and not need it than need it and not have the courage to leave you alone."

"But you thought . . . you thought . . ."

"I hoped." When she didn't reply, he added, "I didn't think you'd be unwilling."

"I don't think we should see each other anymore. I will *not* get involved."

"Addy . . ."

She stood up. "I'll get your coat." She marched out to the entrance hall, took his coat from its hanger, and stood there, holding it for him. All the time he was rolling down his sleeves and putting on his jacket, she didn't say one word or look at him. He took the coat from her hands, watching her as he put it on, then said in a low voice, "Good night, Addy. I'll be in touch."

She didn't reply as he left.

CHAPTER SEVEN

IN THE DAYS that followed, Addy's designs changed again. She'd been creating wondrously romantic gowns, soft and feminine, for the fall show due in two months, but now she drew suits in somber colors with high collars of sturdy material. They were fabulous but stark.

"A marvelous contrast, Addy," Miss Pru commented. "I don't believe you've ever had such an interesting variety in one show before." Miss Pru was choosing which model would wear what for the showing. The seamstress would then sew it to that model's measurements. She was trying to discourage Pearl, who was begging to wear the vertical-black-and-white-striped robe. "You'd look twelve feet tall!" Miss Pru protested.

"That's only two feet taller than I already am," Pearl boasted. The seamstress whose sole work was to make up the samples for the shows also exclaimed how unusual the designs were. To herself Addy called them B.I.H. and A.I.H., for before and after ice-hockey night. Why she chose to blame the ice hockey for the steamy confrontation by the fireplace in the parlor was not something she dwelt on.

Sam had no regard for her rejection at all. He'd dropped by to see Grendel a couple of times, and once he returned her from a photography session. Addy was filled with jealousy at the thought that Sam had seen Diana Hunter. Diana really was a huntress, she concluded, an insidiously clever one who was charming and very nice-looking, who hid her predatory ways behind a friendly facade. On dark nights she probably smiled with pointed teeth, and her fingernails grew into claws. She was a leopard who could change her spots, a fit mate for a panther.

Sam also came with his mother for her additional fittings and chatted with a tongue-tied Addy as if they were old friends. He might feel comfortable, but she was a basket case. She darted peeks at his mouth and remembered . . . She glanced at his hands and thought . . . She stared at his hard, wide chest and knew . . . She struggled to keep her breath steady and her chest from swelling and her hands from trembling. She was in agony.

Sam met Marcus, who eyed him noncommittally and said, "You the one got in the ladies-only show that time? The watcher saw the doctor's tab on your car license plate and let you in."

Addy gasped. "What did you do to him?"

"He watches closer now."

Sam regarded Marcus with intense interest. "I know all about you, Mr. Freeman," he began pleasantly. But

Marcus shot him a glance that stilled his tongue and made Addy very curious.

The models met for fittings for the fall show. Patty-cake danced in to exclaim, "I've got a part in a play! It'll open this fall!" She was so excited no one could get another thought through to her.

Dark-haired Linda informed them, "I found an extra job as a go-go dancer. I'm making more there than as a legal secretary!"

Naturally they all waited to hear what news redheaded Dale came up with, but she had no news at all. They all scolded her for being dull and claimed that her life was too prosaic. She just smiled lazily.

The blonde, brunette, redhead, and one black Pearl had their fittings and loved the new clothes. They moved in front of the mirrors and told Addy the clothes were smashing.

But their compliments gave her no particular joy. She was pale and said "Thank you" in a nice, polite voice, but they weren't paying any attention to her and didn't see that she was suffering.

Sam saw and was tender with her. "Quit being so kind to me!" she snarled at him under her breath.

"Why?" he asked.

"I can't handle kindness." She hadn't had much practice.

"I can use a lot... any you might have lying around ...even crumbs." His voice was low and coaxing...and kind.

"Cut it out!" she snapped, flouncing away from him.

At another fitting a few days later, Mrs. Harrow said to Addy, "Sam is a very nice boy, and my favorite son. Of course, he's the only son I have." Addy recognized that old chestnut and smiled politely.

"Addy, why won't you date Sam? He's harmless."

Which just showed how little Mrs. Harrow knew about her own son! Harmless? Sam? Balderdash! He should wear a warning sign. "Mrs. Harrow," Addy replied carefully, not looking at her, her face feeling pinched with the effort, "Grendel is illegitimate."

"My third daughter almost was," Mrs. Harrow told Addy conversationally, "but the divorce became final, and I got married to her father just in the nick of time."

Addy could only stare.

"Of course, her father stood by me. He was excessively possessive, and I had a married name at the time. But everyone knew who the father was, and that's why my first husband was so asinine about the divorce. He wanted things to be awkward for me out of revenge. My second husband, Tom, never told me how much he paid my first husband to let me have the divorce. I was sure at the time that everyone in Indianapolis was pointing at me and whispering behind their hands about me. It was an extremely nerve-racking time.

"She's a darling. I'm so glad we have her," Mrs. Harrow went on. "She was worth all the mess. We named her Cyn, which shows you Tom's humor. It was so long ago and I've been married so many times and have so many children and stepchildren that the scandal is almost buried. Only my oldest enemies remember and recall it. Times change. I wouldn't worry about it if I were you."

"No wonder Sam is so understanding about it."

"Oh, Sam." Mrs. Harrow flapped a dismissive hand. "He's a pushover for babies. Always has been. Baby *anything*, but human babies especially. That's why he's chosen the field he has. But he's never been serious about a woman. I've been pushing and prodding, but he says for me to be patient, he's working on it." Mrs. Harrow eyed Addy in a penetrating way, then she smiled and spoke of other things.

* * *

A day or so later, when Sam came by and invited Addy to dinner, she groused, "You certainly have a great deal of free time."

"That's why I'm a pediatric consultant. Do you realize I went to school until I was thirty-two? That's a lot of years to study, but the rewards are large fees and no office hours."

"No office?"

"No. The patients I see are almost always in a hospital. Occasionally I see some who aren't, but then I meet them in their home or at their doctor's office."

"How do they get in touch with you?"

"I have an answering service that always knows exactly where I am. I rarely have emergencies." He paused and smiled at her. "Addy, come to dinner with me tonight. I'll take you wherever you want to go."

"I can't. If you walk on the track, you get hit by the train."

"I'm a train?"

"Something like that." She examined her thumbnail. "Sam, give it up. I'm not interested."

"You don't kiss 'not interested.'"

"Well. Yes. I don't know why that is, but . . . you are very good."

"That's a start," Sam told her.

She was scornful. "It's all men want. Sex."

"You've known the wrong men."

"Man. One man."

"One?" He could only stand and look at her.

By that time she'd given her thumb as much attention as any thumb deserves in a month, so she flicked a glance at Sam and said good-bye and walked away from him.

* * *

Two days after that, in the late afternoon, Miss Pru came to Addy in her attic studio and said Sam needed her. Irritated, Addy set the timer and told the loitering Emmaline to remove the material from the color bath and rinse it when the dinger sounded. Emmaline nodded in her lazy, slow way, and Addy sighed in exasperation and clattered down the stairs to the second floor and then down the grand staircase and through to the front parlor.

Sam looked as if he'd been on a three-day drunk. He needed a shave, he was hunched down on the sofa with his elbows on his thighs and his hands hanging between his knees, and he was staring at the floor. He hadn't taken off his coat. His hair was tousled, as if his hands had raked through it a hundred times. He didn't respond when Addy spoke to him.

She walked slowly toward him and stood in front of him, but he didn't look up. She knelt down and put her hands on his knees, peering into his face. Wearily he met her eyes and sighed as he almost shook his head. It was as if he'd started to but didn't have the energy to complete the movement, or that he'd shaken it so much that the muscles were exhausted.

She touched his stubbled cheek, her heart filled with compassion as she asked in a whisper, "What is it?"

"It's never easy." His throat sounded raw.

"No?" she encouraged.

"We lost a hard one. Something should have worked. It shouldn't have happened. We did nothing wrong. But we lost."

"Oh, Sam . . ." And she kissed his cheek with infinite tenderness.

"There are so many things I don't understand. God is going to run when I get to heaven, I have so many 'whys' to ask him. Everything has a reason. The universe is logical. But I can't figure out this one. It's another one in which there is no sane reason why we lost him. That little tiny life just . . . snuffed out. And there isn't one good reason for it."

As Addy listened, she gently pushed his coat off his shoulders and pulled the sleeves from his arms. His rumpled suit coat followed, then his tie. Miss Pru arrived with an omelet and a glass of warm milk with vanilla and nutmeg mixed in it. "I imagine you've had too much coffee," she said.

Sam nodded. He ate, chewing, waving the fork, going over the diagnosis, the treatments, exactly what had happened and when, and asking why it had. Addy listened.

Then when he yawned and sank into a stupor, she took his hand and led him up the grand staircase. She gave him a terry-cloth robe and showed him the bathroom, saying, "Hot shower." Then she made up the bed in an empty room and turned on the electric blanket. Outside it was snowing again.

He came into the room, heavy-eyed and rough-looking, his hair wet. She got a fresh towel and sat him on the edge of the bed and dried his hair. He wrapped his arms around her and leaned his head against her, moving his face tiredly against her soft breasts. She told him softly to stop it. He ignored her.

His hands turned hard and demanding, and he pulled her down on his lap to hold her and kiss her. There was no denying him. Her resistance was only tentative. Before long she was lying on the bed, allowing him to make love to her. Her clothes vanished as if by magic, and soon they were in the bed, their naked bodies touching.

The sensation of the texture of his hairy skin against her sensitive, quivering body sent her mind reeling. He seemed to feel it too, and held her silently so that they could realize the pleasure it gave them both. "Oh, Addy," he breathed in her ear. The sound, almost inaudible, thrilled her all the way down to her toes. He moved his mouth down her soft throat, deliberately, delicately whiskering her, his mouth opening hotly to kiss and lick along her skin, tasting her.

To feel his scalding, wet mouth within that beard-roughened face was thrilling, and it made her gasp and squirm against him. His body jerked and tensed, while hers softened and relaxed. He kissed her mouth, his hands roaming over her, and she buried her own hands in his tousled hair. His kiss deepened, his mouth opening, moving, encouraging her response. Her lips parted, and their mouths fused.

His strong palms slid over her satin skin lovingly, taking pleasure in the feel of her, and her skin tingled at his touch. Her body moved, inviting his explorations. Their kiss deepened even more, and as their tongues met, his fingers sought her secret places and touched her gently. She moaned, and her breasts swelled against him, aching for his attentions.

Sweat filmed their bodies. He slid easily down her, causing her to gasp. His mouth teased her breasts while his hands smoothed and touched her. Her own hands moved on him, though not as boldly. She ran them greedily through his hair and around his head and throat, along his tightly muscled shoulders and down his rock-hard back. She rubbed his hairy chest and clutched his shoulders as she writhed and moved, wanting him.

She wanted him . . . terribly. She pressed against him, and her hungry mouth kissed wherever it could. Their breath steamed in that cool room, and their bodies were wet with sweat from their passionate labor. Still, Sam prolonged it. Finally he slid back up her, his weight on her. And as he kissed her, his tongue gently invaded her opened mouth and his body invaded hers.

He paused, shifted to his elbows, and breathed heavily

as they lay coupled, clamped together, fused. He looked down into her face. "I love you, Addy." He was breathing hard; his eyes were leaping fires, smoldering and flaming into hers as his body smoldered and flamed in hers.

He leaned down and kissed her very sweetly, then his weight came down on hers and he began their ride to an explosion that lifted them to an exquisite release. Addy clutched him, crying out in exultation as her body tensed against the tide, then she fell back, limp and filled with wonder.

He lay on her, his elbows again supporting most of his weight, and showered tiny kisses onto her flushed face. In a slow, rough, thickened voice, he said, "Fabulous. My God, I've never had it like that. Dear God. Oh, Addy."

He lifted himself carefully off her and lay beside her to gather her close. "Let me sleep just a minute. I want you again right away. I just have to sleep for a little while. Don't move . . ." And he went instantly to sleep.

Addy lay in his arms, stunned from the amazing experience. It was astounding! So that's how it could be. She could not refrain from touching him. He was so deep in sleep that her gentle fingers made no impression on him. She touched his lips in something like awe. She smoothed back his hair with gentle soothings. So that's how it could be between a man and a woman. It was marvelous. It was a miracle. Why hadn't it been that way with Paul?

He had been inept, selfish, and she hadn't desired him. She hadn't wanted him because she hadn't loved him. And she knew now she was in love with Samuel Grady, this terrible, marvelous man. She lay in his arms, touching him, yearning for him. But after a time, she carefully moved away from him and stood naked beside the bed. She looked down at him, and her heart moved.

She dressed pensively, finding her clothes scattered around the room where he'd flung them. She looked down at his sleeping face many times. She hesitated long in the doorway, then went out, closing it softly behind her.

Downstairs in her office, she sat at her cluttered desk and gazed out the window with unseeing eyes. Miss Pru found her there.

"Adelina, what are you up to?" She didn't say it with censure but with concern.

"I don't know." Addy turned troubled eyes to Miss Pru.

"I'd hate to think you'd be . . ."

"What?"

"Well . . . indiscreet," Miss Pru supplied. "I'd hate for you to be hurt."

"He was so . . ."

"I don't mean to interfere." Miss Pru turned away.

"No one has a better right."

The two women looked at each other, and Addy got up and went to the older woman and put her arms around her. They stood silently, then Miss Pru patted her shoulder and left the room.

At dinnertime Addy checked on Sam, but he hadn't even moved. She looked in on him again before going to bed, leaving a glass of milk with a saucer over it and a wrapped sandwich on a tray in case he woke up hungry. His clothes had been pressed, his shirt was washed and ironed, and they were hung on hangers where he could readily see them.

In the morning he was still asleep. The bed was rumpled and he was in a sprawled position. Addy stood for a while, filling her eyes with the sight of him, then took the untouched tray of food and, leaving his door open, went down to the kitchen. She left the door to the stairwell open too. Then she fried bacon and put rolls in the oven. When he arrived a few minutes later the coffee had just finished perking. She looked over her shoulder at him shyly.

He grinned at her and said, "Good morning, darling." She moved from his embrace, embarrassed. "You are an angel of mercy," he told her.

"For letting the aroma of eggs and bacon and coffee float up the back stairs?"

"Well . . . It's the second best way to waken a man."

"Second?" she began, then stopped as he grinned. "How do you feel?" she asked, changing the subject.

"I was out on my feet. Jeremy and I had been with the parents, trying to help them cope, from midnight until just before I came to you. I couldn't think about anything but getting to you. I was used up and needed you. Oh, Addy, you were so sweet to me."

She hadn't yet solved how she was going to handle what had happened between them, so she said briskly, "You start with oatmeal."

"I can eat," he admitted ruefully, "but I'm not hungry for food."

"I'm not getting involved with you," she warned him.

"Honey, you're already involved with me." She again evaded his reaching hands and looked up at him forlornly. "It'll be all right," he assured her. "Just leave everything to me." He'd been completely exhausted the day before, but she saw that the loving and the long sleep had restored him. He was his old self—confident, teasing, and kind.

Grendel bounced in just then, exhilarated to find Sam there. She asked to be held and exclaimed over his whiskers, so he brushed them against her cheek. She shrieked and giggled and wriggled in his arms, and he laughed.

Addy envied her daughter. Then Grendel squealed, "Mommy, did you feel his whis-pers?"

"Whis-*kers*," Addy corrected, standing aloof and busy at the stove.

"Did you *feel* them?"

Sam looked at Grendel with a solemn expression and asked, "Do you think your mommy should be whiskered too?"

"Yes!" Grendel yelled, chortling.

"Behave!" Addy commanded. "I'm cooking the eggs." But Sam went up behind her and hugged her, and his touch sent electric thrills all through her. An egg hit the floor with a splat.

Holding her against him, Sam nuzzled her neck as she scolded, "The egg!" That made him laugh, while Grendel squealed and yelled.

Miss Pru entered with raised eyebrows and a hidden smile. "Shall I whisker you too?" Sam offered.

She put up a cheek quite willingly, and he bent down and rubbed his against it in a courtly way. She patted his prickly cheek and said, "Ahhh, that was just lovely."

Grendel disagreed with Miss Pru. "It's *funny!*"

Addy didn't comment about her own reaction. She just bent down to mop up the egg—as Sam reached over and turned off the smoking skillet.

He was full of himself this morning. Every move was one of triumph. He was the conqueror.

Addy couldn't handle the whole situation. She was embarrassed. Making love was extremely intimate, and she was back to not quite looking at him. She couldn't possibly regret what had happened; it had been too glorious. To know at last how it could be between a man and a woman making love was the stuff of dreams. But... but she'd gone quite wild. Would he remember? Had he been aware of her conduct? He'd been so intense himself, perhaps he hadn't realized she'd been out of control.

He did remember. His dancing eyes told her so every time she almost looked at him. She kept her mouth prim and her back straight all through breakfast while she longed for him to take her back upstairs, strip off her clothes, take her to bed, and rub her entire body with his whiskery face. She swallowed a lot and licked her lips with quick flicks, trying to keep her eyes on her plate. And when he left to go to his apartment to shave, he said, "Keep my bed turned down, Tiger."

"Now, just a—" she began, but he only gave her mouth a hard, possessive kiss and went out the door to his car, whistling. She stood in the ever-glowing light of the Edison bulb in the entrance hall and leaned her head against the cold pane and wondered how she'd ever gotten so tangled up with Sam Grady. The train was looming ahead, and there was no time to get off the track.

She dragged herself upstairs to the attic, which she'd left to Emmaline the day before, and stopped in the door. On the drying line were four batik cloths, each a yard square. The spidery lines and various colors were stunning. Emmaline looked up placidly, and Addy stared at her. "Emmaline?" she asked uncertainly, gesturing at the fantastic artwork.

Emmaline looked at them vaguely, then smiled and went back to spreading wax on another cloth, not bothering to reply.

Addy examined them more closely. "Did *you* do these?" she demanded, stunned into incomprehension.

Emmaline looked up again and nodded before going back to her new design. "Umm-hmm," she said.

"They're *gorgeous!*"

Emmaline smiled without looking up. "Thanks."

"And I've kept you chained to that sewing machine when you can do something like *this!*" Addy was appalled.

"You don't mind?" Emmaline slid the cloth into a color bath.

"*Mind?* I'm going to bring the chains up here! Do you know what these could sell for?" She seemed to see dollar signs in front of her eyes. "We'll have to talk to Marcus. We need to set you up in business. You can work here until you get started. Then you can have your own business, and I'll buy from you. Can you give me first refusal? These are *fantastic!*" She was awed. "They're so beautiful, they almost scare me. I'll find Marcus."

"He's out of town," Emmaline offered absently.

"Where?"

"I don't know." She didn't sound interested.

"Probably in Chicago taking lessons from the Mob."

"Yeah," Emmaline agreed indifferently.

Addy went a little berserk. She ran for samples and matched them with the cloths, pairing various dresses with the scarves. She sketched up her ideas, then made a list of women to invite to come see them. "How many can you make in a day?"

"I don't know." Emmaline shrugged.

"Don't press..."

"Not 'til they're dry," she agreed.

"I mean don't hurry them. Do them at your own pace." Addy tried to think how to be clear. "Do them the way you do your seams for dresses. Don't hurry."

"All right."

Addy looked to see what she was working on as Emmaline India-inked a Chinese character in the middle of a hand-drawn, perfect circle. Then she took a smaller brush and added the perfect finishing drip mark. Addy was dumbfounded. "Emmaline, where did you learn to do that?"

"Oh...on public television. They had a show on people treasures...uh...the country says these people are treasures..."

"National treasures," Addy supplied, remembering seeing the same show.

"And this lady did dresses like this."

"My lord." Addy sat down on a stool. *"You* are a treasure."

Emmaline smiled and scoffed, "I'm too young, Addy. They were all old. Probably thirty-five or even forty."

"You're a young treasure," Addy assured her.

"Aw, Addy, you're always so nice."

And Addy blushed as she remembered how often she'd complained about Emmaline to Marcus.

But the day wasn't over.

The mail had come as usual. Miss Pru sorted it. As happened routinely each day, she put Addy's mail on the credenza in her office. There was rarely anything earthshaking in the mail and therefore no particular need to open it immediately, so Addy left it there until just after lunch.

There was one letter, an ordinary letter. Nothing about it indicated that it was different. It was from California, she noted before slitting it open. It was addressed to her as a personal letter, and it was from Paul Morris.

CHAPTER EIGHT

EVEN THOUGH SHE'D glanced at the signature and read the "Paul," Addy didn't really believe it was from Paul Morris. But her body became very still as she read the note without actually absorbing the words. She had to read it several times before she really understood that it *was* Paul who'd written, and what it was that he'd said.

"I know you'll be surprised to hear from me. I thought about you a couple of times after I left and wondered how you got along.

"I got a copy of the *Journal* a while back and saw the picture of a little girl named Grendel Kildaire. Kildaire isn't a common name, and it said her mother was a designer and that's what your masters was, so I decided to write and find out if you kept the kid and if she's mine.

"She's about the right age and she looks like all the kids in my family. You can write me here. Paul."

Addy's emotions ran from shock at hearing from him after such a long time, to indignation that he'd had the nerve to write to her, to fury that he'd dare to ask if the child was *his!* She released an animal roar, a mixture of maternal protection, the humiliation she'd endured, and the burden of worry and loneliness of the last four years. It was a primal crying out against all the injustice of the abandonment she'd endured at his hands.

Miss Pru hurried in just as Addy was tearing the letter apart in the first act of destroying her enemy. The sharp cry of "Adelina!" stopped her. She raised almost mad eyes to Miss Pru, not recognizing her. The older woman said her name again, but the tone was gentle, reaching out to her.

Addy turned stark, staring eyes to Miss Pru and just looked at her, as if seeing safety in a storm-tossed sea. Miss Pru lifted a slow hand to her arm and asked, "What is it?"

Addy stared down at the ripped page in her hand. As understanding returned, she held her rigid hands out toward Miss Pru, who took the pieces from Addy's stiffened fingers, then went to the desk to fit the pieces together so that she could read it.

When she'd done that, she looked at Addy and said gently, "I won't say anything right now. It will be better if I think about my words first."

Addy stood stock still, every muscle rigid. "She isn't *his*. She's *mine!*"

"Yes, dear, I know. Let me think about this," Miss Pru said placatingly.

"How dare he!" Addy trembled with fury.

"That's true, Addy, but not about the note. It's true of some of Paul's conduct. But let's calm ourselves and not say or do anything rash. Let's just put this aside until we can think clearly."

"I don't need to think! Not about this." She jerked her hand in the air.

Calmly Miss Pru took Scotch tape and repaired the letter. Then, as Addy stood there like a stone statue, Miss Pru read it silently again. She put the letter inside a folder, out of sight. "I'll put this in the file cabinet of business letters, under 'M' for Morris."

"How about 'R' for rat?" Addy snapped.

"Or we could put it under 'W' for weasel." Miss Pru tendered a small, coaxing smile.

Addy would have none of it. "'B' for bastard!" she snarled.

Miss Pru nodded, raising her eyebrows with a thoughtful expression. "That's a fairly accurate description," she agreed.

Through her teeth, Addy growled, "He thought about me 'a couple of times'!"

"Yes." Miss Pru's voice was soft and comforting. "I know."

"How dare he?" Addy raged. "He takes off, leaving me with the consequences of his lust, and he thinks about me 'a couple of times'!"

"It's been a shock, hearing this way," she offered.

"After all you and I had to go through just because of him!"

"But some good came of it, Addy. We have Grendel. And I found you. My life was so empty before you came to my house."

"Look what it did to my parents. What would have happened to Grendel and me if we hadn't found you?"

"Well, it would have been extremely dull for me, I'll tell you that!" And Miss Pru smiled again.

Addy walked stiffly to the window and stood staring

out at the woods. The temperature was edging up into the low thirties, turning yesterday's brief snow into slush.

"Would you like me to ask Sam to come over?" Miss Pru suggested. "He's very sensible and—"

"No! I've had enough of men. Look what being with a man has done to our lives."

"You don't... regret keeping Grendel, do you?"

Addy's head whipped around, and she glowered at Miss Pru. "Of course not!" she snapped. "How could you ever think that?"

"Then you can't resent Paul..." Miss Pru began.

"It was ghastly... being with him. So embarrassing. So intimate! It was terrible."

"You're primarily upset that he left you," Miss Pru went on.

"That's right! The bastard. I could wring his neck!"

"Addy!" Miss Pru managed to almost frown as she straightened and tried hopelessly to look formidable.

"Sorry." But Addy was sulky and her response came automatically. She wasn't really contrite.

Again picking up the thread of her evaluation of Addy's conflict, Miss Pru said, "You don't resent becoming pregnant and having Grendel as much as you're insulted that Paul would leave you to solve your problem all by yourself."

"And writing four years later and asking, 'Hey, is that my kid?' You're darned right I resent him. Insulted? That's not quite the word. At the time I was horrified, trapped, devastated, embarrassed... All those things, and on top of it all I had to face my parents and tell them. It tore me in two. I still haven't healed, and I doubt my parents ever will."

"I know it was very difficult for all of you."

"But you didn't judge me," Addy pointed out.

"My love, don't you see that I was in a unique position? I needed only to judge you according to my own ideas. Your parents judged not only you but also themselves. Don't you see they can't forgive *themselves?* They still feel they failed you. Grendel reminds them of that.

"People are extremely complicated," Miss Pru went on. "Body language is supposed to be a science and you can 'read' someone by the way they sit or stand or move their facial muscles. To me that's too much like Freud, who said the mind was conditioned and driven by sex.

"To say sex alone is responsible for our behavior is like the six blind men touching the elephant. One felt the tail and said an elephant was like a rope. One fingered the tusk and said a heavy spear. Another, handling the ear, said it was like a leaf. And the one who felt the leg said it was a tree. 'No,' said the one at the trunk, 'it's a snake.' And the one who touched the side said an elephant was a large wall. They were all right.

"The mind's that way—very large and diverse. How can we tell what influences the way people react? A person doesn't talk or listen on one level. You listen to another person speak, plan what to reply, are reminded of something else entirely, and your thoughts go along on an altogether different course.

"You may cross a leg one way because of pain, or a twinge of gas, or a body hair caught on your underwear. There are too many levels all working at once to guess why anyone does anything. Our minds are too complex and busy. We try to oversimplify."

"But people go into therapy to find out why they do things."

"We might discover something there, a comfortable reason, and if we do, fine. But the real reason could be lost because it was such a silly thing, so meaningless, so casually said or seen that it doesn't make an individual impression. It just sank into our busy brain and perhaps touched something else, which then influenced how we see ourselves in the mirror, or what part of ourselves, or how we see our children."

Addy capsuled it: "So everyone should just do his own thing and forget about agonizing over how other people will react."

"No, no, no." Miss Pru shook her head and lifted a staying hand. "No one can do that and you know it. I sometimes think you come up with ideas like that just to raise my dander." She studied Addy carefully. "Rules can be silly, but you can count on the golden one, doing unto others as you would have them do unto you. And the big ten are superb guidelines, though most of those are incorporated into the golden one. And, Addy, that one is good to keep in mind as you consider Paul's letter."

Addy's look turned hostile, but Miss Pru smiled gently and said, "I'll file this under 'M.' It doesn't have to be dealt with today." She turned at the door. "Did you see Emmaline's batiks? Aren't they gorgeous?"

"Oh, Miss Pru, and I've treated her so badly."

"See? Body language. You thought she was lazy, but she's a dreamer of beautiful things."

"And the colors! They're exquisite."

"Are you going to use them?" Miss Pru asked gently.

"Oh, yes! I thought I'd do simple frocks of solid colors so that the scarves will star."

"Excellent. Have you chosen any of the samples?"

"Several. A couple will be garish, and we'll have to make sure only women who they flatter buy them. You'll have to do that. Your color sense is staggering."

"Oh? Let me see," Miss Pru said, and they began to leave the office, pausing only long enough for Miss Pru to file the folder under 'M.' They climbed to the attic to gawk and exclaim over Emmaline's art treasures.

So the letter was put aside, but Addy didn't forget it. It haunted her. And her determination to shun Paul and spurn any attempt to contact Grendel was solidified.

Sam arrived in time for dinner that evening. He carried two cases into the house—his medical bag and another small one. He also brought Miss Pru a hostess plant, and she said she'd start a greenhouse if he kept that up.

When Addy gave him a cold stare, he grinned at her in encouragement, but he didn't try to take her in his arms.

At the table, Miss Pru set another place, and Grendel hopped around like a cricket. It was very homey. The great big house, the aroma of good cooking, the bright faces—though Addy knew hers was sour—all created a feeling of constancy and security.

"We have a hard freeze coming up." Sam offered that bit of news. "But it shouldn't last. March came in like a lion and therefore it will have to go out like a lamb."

"I've got a new book," Miss Pru murmured. "I'll just crawl into bed and read."

Grendel went under the kitchen table and growled, pretending to be the March lion. Sam squatted down and asked her, "Are you a bunny?"

"Noooooo!"

He thought elaborately and asked, "Are you a bird?"

"Noooooo!" Grendel had to smother giggles with her hand.

"Well, what in the world *are* you?"

"A fear-OOO-shus *lion!*"

Sam hit his forehead with the flat of his palm and said, "Of course!"

Addy went stiffly about, doing her share of the chores and giving Miss Pru disapproving glances for making Sam feel so welcome. Miss Pru ignored her.

During dinner, Miss Pru mentioned Emmaline's batiks and suggested, "Sam, you'll want to see them."

When he agreed, Miss Pru should have flown backward clear down the hall with the force of the furious glance Addy sent her. Instead she just smiled.

Addy figured that maybe Sam would forget Miss Pru's suggestion, but he didn't. After the dishwasher was loaded and humming, Sam said, "I'd really like to see what Emmaline has been up to. How about now?"

"Ask Miss Pru," Addy said stiffly.

"Why would I climb two flights of stairs when I have a young lady who'll volunteer?" Miss Pru pinched Addy's bottom and hissed for her to behave herself.

Addy led Sam sullenly toward the more formal grand staircase at the entrance. To use the back stairs would be including him too informally. He paused briefly, but she went up the stairs in measured steps as if to a firing squad. He took the steps two at a time and caught up with her. "When Grendel gets married, it'll have to be here," he decided.

She gave him a stern, quelling flick of a stare to show him that how or where Grendel was married was none of his affair. He might still be feeling squashily sentimental after tossing her in bed the day before, but she herself was feeling daggers through her vitals from Paul's letter.

Sam stopped on the second floor and told her he'd be back in just a minute. He had to, as he informed her, "put my shaving kit in my room."

"*Your* room!" she exploded.

But he strode off, entered the room he'd slept in the day before, and came out, grinning at her as he closed the door. "The bed's stripped. Clean sheets every day?"

Carefully spacing the words, she said gratingly, "You are not moving in here."

"Oh," he said, and his face was puzzled. "Well, at least the next time I'd have shaving things here, and I wouldn't have to go down to breakfast all whiskery. Of course, you all did seem to enjoy the whiskers. I could wait to shave them off until just before I had to leave the house."

"There will be no next time. You are not going to stay here at all!"

"No one can predict anything." He smiled at her confidently. Then he glanced around. "Where're the stairs?"

She wanted to settle once and for all that the room was not his, but he took her arm, and she gestured automatically toward the door to the attic stairs. She was gathering the proper argument when he kissed her mouth, and the words scattered off in all directions. While she was furiously searching for them again, she had to try to push down the waves of desire his kiss had exploded inside her.

By that time they were up the attic stairs. Sam reached around her to open the door, leaning so close that she breathed the male scent of him. Her senses were affected in such a swooning, irrational way that she stumbled.

He steadied her, grinned down at her, and kissed her again. Then he looked around, apparently not at all affected by her kisses the way she was by his. She seized on that thought and worried over it. Why wasn't he equally affected?

Sam whistled, impressed with the batiks. "The girls have to see these."

"What girls?" Addy retorted waspishly. All of his harem?

Absently, engrossed in the beautiful scarves, he replied, "My sisters."

"Oh," she said feebly.

"This is Ann." He touched one. "That's Cyn." He

pointed to another. "And...that's Terry." He nodded toward his last choice.

She became indignant. "I want that one."

"No." He was positive. "This one is you. I saw it as soon as I opened the door."

"That one?" She eyed it, astonished.

"It's complicated and subtle, the way you are. And it's beautiful." He turned to her. "The way you are." He kissed her just as beautifully.

That was when she should have jerked back and taken a firm stand about the room he was appropriating downstairs and his place *outside* her life. It was the best time to present a clear, concise admonition. The knowledge that it was the right time did cross her mind fleetingly. But with his kiss, she lost track of what she was supposed to be firm about. She had a fragmented idea that she could come back to it and get it all sorted out later. After that she drowned in his kiss.

He was really very good at kissing. She excused her participation by thinking that, when you find someone that good, you should appreciate it as you would fine music or dazzling colors. You need to give your attention to such talent and relish and enjoy. She did that.

Finally he paused and smiled, just above her face and out of focus. "Do I get clean sheets every night?" he whispered. She couldn't remember why they would have to go to all the trouble of putting clean sheets down on the studio floor; it was only a little dusty. But before she could start to undress him to make love, he asked softly, "What could I have done or said to make you so cross with me?"

It was like splashing a bucket of cold water over her. Paul rushed back to her mind. She jerked free and tried to recall the words she needed to make it clear that Sam was not going to become a part of her life.

"Sam," she began, but instead of looking serious and subdued, he smiled down at her with great tenderness and reached to take her hand. She jerked it away from him. "You are not moving in here. You go right this minute and get that shaving kit out of that room. That room is not yours. I am not a convenient lay for you just because you need sex and haven't the control—"

"Hey. What's up?"

That flustered her, and she had to straighten out her tongue in order to continue. "I will not go to bed with you, so just forget it."

"What happened? Something's wrong. I'm almost sure I haven't said anything. If I did, I didn't intend to put you on your ear. It has to be someone else. Who said what?" His concern was irritatingly sweet.

"No one said anything. It's just that I don't want to get involved with any man."

"I didn't hurt you, did I? I tried to be gentle with you, but God, Addy, you were fantastic and I—"

"No, no," she interrupted, "you didn't do anything." She looked at him, feeling full of hurt, and admitted, "It was lovely, but . . ."

"Then did I say anything? Honey, I'm on your side all the way. I can't think of anything I might have said that could've made you unhappy—"

"No, you've been very sweet and I—"

"Then it was someone else." His eyes questioned her solemnly as he promised, "I'll break his neck. Who was it?"

"It's just . . . Sam, I just don't want any kind of a relationship."

"Is it *all* men or just me?"

"Oh, Sam, it isn't anything to do with you."

"It has everything to do with me."

"I feel terrible about this. I shouldn't have—"

"I don't feel much like laughing myself right now."

"Sam..." She was almost pleading instead of being firm.

"You have to tell me what it is. How can I fix it until I know what's wrong? Tell me who's hurt you." His low voice coaxed her. "Remember, I can damn near fix anything."

She might have told him then except that she and Miss Pru had shoved the threat of Paul into a file drawer so that he wouldn't loom so badly. She just couldn't cope with her feelings for Sam. He was too devastating. Her feelings for him threatened to swamp her at a time when she needed a clear head to deal with the threat of Paul. She'd always handled and solved her own problems. In spite of Miss Pru, Addy felt she was alone in the world and Grendel's only protection.

"My interest in you isn't a casual interlude," Sam told her. "I'm serious about you, Addy. I'm so serious about you that I'm willing to back off and take it easy until you're ready to consider how much I do care. We'll be friends in the meantime. All right?"

Not believing he could be serious, she eyed him cautiously, but his face was very earnest. Their eyes locked, and she knew that, although she might not be able to handle an intimate affair with him just yet, she didn't want to lose him. She held out her hand. He lifted it to his heart and, his eyes steady on her, ventured, "Friends can kiss."

She gave him a wan smile. He leaned forward and very gently kissed her mouth in undemanding sympathy. It almost wrecked her.

CHAPTER NINE

THE NEXT AFTERNOON Diana Hunter called to say that the sleet was so bad she was going to stay at the studio and not even try to go home. Was it all right for Grendel to stay too? Addy said yes. But just after six, when Sam arrived, Diana called again to say that Grendel was running a fever and what did one do with a child who was sick?

Sam said he'd take Addy to Diana's studio and bring Grendel home. On the way there, Addy sat rigidly still, amazed by Sam's skill in driving on the slick streets. When they arrived at Diana's, Sam wouldn't let Addy needlessly risk the walk and made her sit in the car while he went inside. He came out carrying a bundled-up Grendel, whom he put carefully on Addy's lap for the drive home.

He was so skilled on the ice that Addy didn't realize he was deliberately exaggerating the road conditions. When they turned into her deserted street, the car slid sideways for a heart-stopping fifty feet or so. He allowed it to creep into her driveway and slide to a calculated stop. He grinned at her. "Whew! Wasn't that a lot of fun?" He laughed when she grimaced. Then he said, "It's a good thing I left my shaving kit here. I believe you wouldn't turn a knight out on a dog like this." She gave him a hesitant look as he slid out of the car. He insisted Addy stay there while he carried Grendel into the house. Then he came back for Addy.

He hadn't exaggerated the difficulty in walking. It was treacherous. She accepted the fact that he would have to stay the night.

All evening long Addy was quiet, distracted, and aloof, although Grendel's temperature didn't frighten her. They had put her to bed and made her comfortable. Grendel did her best to seem pitiful. She raised a tiny hand to her forehead and let out languishing sighs. Sam predicted a cold was in the offing. He recommended a nice glass of orange juice and cautioned Addy not to overdo the vitamin C. Addy only muttered, "What do you know?" as she mashed up another vitamin C pill and dumped it into the orange juice.

For dinner Miss Pru served sausage patties, baked potatoes, green beans, carrots, and applesauce with hot biscuits and honey. Sam smiled like a large cat that's been stroked and patted his stomach as he told Addy to convey his compliments to the chef, who sat across the table and smirked. Addy decided Grendel had absorbed her dramatics by osmosis from Miss Pru.

They'd almost finished eating when Grendel appeared like a waif in the doorway from the back stairs. She stood there until they'd all seen her, then said forlornly that she was lonely upstairs...all by herself. She assumed the expression of an abandoned child. Addy wondered if the worn teddy bear, dangling to the floor from one hand, was a calculated touch. Surely Grendel was too young to be that deliberately theatrical.

"Maybe you're not lonely," Addy suggested. "Maybe you're just hungry. Perhaps what you need is some applesauce? And how about a nice hot biscuit with some honey?"

Grendel tried to keep her pose, but a grin crept over her face and she said, "Yes!" She scrambled to her chair and climbed up on it while Addy adroitly slid her padded seat under her. Grendel smiled around the table, ready for the party.

Addy watched her child covertly, knowing she was the most charming and delightful little girl in all the world. But she monitored Grendel's behavior, giving her a ready smile, a slight shake of her head, or a cautioning *shhh* in order to keep her from taking over. Grendel was so darling, it would be easy for Addy to indulge her.

Feeling Sam's eyes on her, Addy sometimes sneaked a glance at him. His smile held such approval that her eyes fled from his.

After the meal he helped clear the table as if he was family, choosing what to give Grendel to help carry to the kitchen.

Then Sam picked her up and carried her back upstairs to her room. He hadn't asked Addy if that was what she wanted him to do, and she sent a resentful glare at his retreating back. He'd even used the back stairs.

Not long after that the furnace went off. Addy heard its dying shudder in the kitchen and locked eyes with Miss Pru, appalled. Addy instantly went to the phone to call Marcus.

The Freeman phone was picked up and, since there

was no reply, Addy knew it was Hedda. "Oh, Hedda, the furnace just quit, and Grendel's sick, and it's so cold. But it's so icy outside. Is there any way at all that Marcus can come over?" There was a pause, then the phone was quietly replaced.

Addy hung up and looked around at a sound from the back hall. Followed by the slippered, robed Grendel, Sam had come down the back stairs. "That sounded like the last gasp of the last mammoth. The furnace?"

The women nodded. He looked around the kitchen, then back into the hall. "Where's the basement door?"

"Can you fix it?" Addy asked doubtfully.

He gave her a clear-eyed, surprised look. "It can't be too different from recalcitrant children, can it? All you have to do is kick it and show it who's boss, right?"

"That's how a pediatric consultant works?"

"Is there another way?"

"He was telling me a story," Grendel said in an accusing tone, as if they'd contrived the interruption.

Sam picked her up and promised, "Right after the furnace is fixed, I'll finish. First things first."

With her arms possessively around Sam's neck, Grendel blinked at Addy. "It's about a darling little girl." Her three-year-old grasp of pronunciation made that "dawing widdle gul."

Addy gave her child a patient look, showed Sam the basement door, and followed him down. There he surveyed the monster, now dead, that took up the middle of the central room. It looked like a giant metal squid with multiple arms which reached into the far recesses of the great house. Sam whistled, impressed. "Has the Smithsonian Institution contacted you about it yet?"

"We've taken only sealed bids, so we're not sure."

Sam walked around it, still carrying Grendel, who also looked around with interest from her comfortable perch in Sam's arms. When he returned to Addy, he handed Grendel to her without a word and opened the door of the somnolent giant. "Umm-humph," he said, then turned to Addy and explained, "My first year of med school there was one whole semester of 'Umm-humph' in all the various ways. Vital class."

"Of course," she agreed seriously as she set Grendel down on the Ping-Pong table.

Sam peered again into the dark vitals of the furnace. The sound of a key at the outside door caused them to turn. The door opened, and another giant descended into the basement. Marcus had arrived like a dark knight to the rescue.

"Oh, Marcus!" Addy exclaimed. "You got here!"

"Thank goodness you were home," she added.

Sam looked offended and said to Marcus, "I hadn't even begun . . ."

Marcus stopped and said, "Oh. You fixing it? Good." Sober-faced, he turned to go.

"Marcus . . ." Addy wailed.

"I'm a *consultant!*" Sam said with asperity.

Marcus turned back. "You intend to check me out?"

Sam sized up the furnace and said, "It can't be too different from people." He waved his arms vaguely. "Body, appendages, heart, lungs . . ."

"And we're going to operate?"

"Never needlessly," Sam replied, holding up an admonishing finger. The two men exchanged smiles. Then Marcus went over, peered inside, squatted down, and looked closer. He stood up and gave a connection a thumping kick . . . and the furnace rumbled back to life.

Addy burst out laughing, and Sam gave her a smug look as he said, "See? I told you all it needed was a good kick."

Marcus raised his shaggy eyebrows and explained,

"It's knowing *where* to kick."

Sam reached out a congratulatory hand and said, "Magnificent. It's always awesome to watch an expert."

Marcus permitted an acknowledging nod and offered, "Want me to help in your next operation?"

"I know too much about you to doubt you could." Sam smiled. "You're a dark horse." But the one who wins the race, Addy thought.

Marcus rolled his eyes and sighed. "You honkies never can resist."

That only made Sam grin wider. "I know you're a mechanical genius. You..."

Before he turned away, Marcus cast Sam a quick look and said, "Keep it to yourself." The words in that soft voice were an order.

"After he tells me," Addy said.

But Marcus only gave Sam another stern glance as he went up the steps to leave.

Addy put out a detaining hand in his direction and called, "I need to talk to you about Emmaline."

Without pausing he called back, "That'll solve itself."

"I think it has," Addy replied.

Marcus turned on the stairs and gave her a level look. "What do you mean?"

"She's a genius. You should see what she can do painting cloth, batiks, silk screening. Good lord, Marcus, you have to come and look!"

"I shall tomorrow. We have dinner guests, and I must return."

"I am so sorry," Addy began to apologize.

"No need to fret, child. I probably saved the furnace from dismemberment at the doctor's hands." Then he told Sam kindly, "Remember, I've had a three-year graduate course in that museum piece. I know all its quirks."

"Mr. Freeman . . ." A small voice came from the Ping-Pong table.

"That you, pixie?"

"You didn't say hello."

"That's 'cause you're a pixie. I can't see you all the time."

"I'm here."

"I see you." He nodded once in formal acknowledgment.

"You can't see me?" Grendel was interested.

Gravely, Marcus explained, "It's like fairies and elves. Can you see them all the time?"

Grendel considered that, her eyes moving as she concentrated. Finally she shook her head. Marcus nodded, turned, and left, then locked the door from the outside.

Addy whirled around to Sam, jumping with curiosity. "How old is he? Do you really know all about him? Does he have enough money? I worry about taking up so much of his time, and he really doesn't charge much, and he generally gives it to someone else. How old is he? Pearl is his daughter, and she's twenty, so he has to be at least forty. Hedda's not his first wife; how many has he had? She's not Pearl's mother. Does she speak at all?"

"Hey!" Sam protested. "He just told me to keep my mouth shut. Would you want me to go back on my word?"

"You didn't give your word."

"I sure did. Marcus only looked at me, but I'll do it his way, and he knows it."

"He is large. But I'm dying to know how old he is."

"Why?"

"I keep trying to figure it out. It would make a difference how I speak to him. I treat him as if he's about your age—"

"I'm not forty!" Sam protested.

"—But if he's older, I shouldn't argue with him quite so much."

"Age gets respect from you?"

"Well, the way I was brought up..." She stopped and blushed. She hadn't been brought up to jump in bed with men either.

"How old are you, Addy?"

"Twenty-seven," she said readily.

"I'm thirty-nine."

She grinned slowly as she raised her eyes to his. "So you're not forty."

"No, I'm not!"

"That's when life begins," she commented.

"Oh, it does, does it? What do you know?"

"I know a lot of women over forty. That's a smashing age for women, and at forty men haven't yet reached their peak."

"Speaking of peaks and perks—" he began.

"Have you ever been married?"

"No." He shook his head a couple of times.

"Why not?" How could he ever have escaped?

"I hadn't yet...met the right one." He lifted his hand to her face and leaned down to kiss her mouth very gently.

Just then a plaintive little voice said, "I'm a little cold."

The adults looked around in surprise, and there sat Grendel in her woolly bathrobe, cross-legged on the Ping-Pong table, watching them. "Where have you been?" Addy asked her.

"Just sitting here...waiting." She sighed theatrically.

"I didn't see you," her mother told her.

"That's 'cause I'm a...patsy?"

"Pixie."

Grendel nodded sagely. "Pixies is hard to see."

Sam picked her up and kissed her forehead. "A cool pixie. Are you hungry?"

"Yes," she said like a child lost in the woods for two weeks who'd survived on berries and bark.

"How about toasted biscuits with jelly and orange juice?"

"Orange juice on biscuits?" A three-year-old can be literal, Addy thought.

"No." Sam was patient. "You put jelly on biscuits and drink orange juice."

That made more sense. With Sam carrying Grendel, they left the metal squid humming in the basement and went up to the kitchen. It was only about eight o'clock. Once Grendel's small personal furnace had been stoked, they took her up the back stairs to her room and tucked her in again. She yawned and yawned and blinked and smiled. She wasn't even trying, and she looked adorable.

Addy allowed herself a brief kiss, touched Grendel's forehead with reassuring fingers, and gave her child a dewy smile. Sam watched Addy, who was gazing at Grendel as she hugged her teddy bear, popped her thumb in her mouth, and sighed, her heavy eyelids closing.

In the hall, Addy and Sam stopped and looked at one another before Sam moved to take Addy into his arms. She remained stiff, her mouth tightening.

"How could you be so cold after that tender, warm scene in Grendel's room?" he complained.

"I'm not going to . . . be with you . . . for the night . . ." The words came out in a jumble.

"For the night?" he questioned.

"I can understand a man your age not being a virgin . . ."

"A virgin?" he asked. "A no-woman's land?"

"But there is no way I'm going to allow you to add

me to your list of convenient women when you feel the urge."

"Urge? As in—"

"And you keep your distance. I know the ice is dangerous, and you may stay this one more time, but in the morning you will pack up your shaving kit and vacate! Do you understand?"

"Urge like for ice cream? Or chocolate?"

"Pearl's chocolate. I'm vanilla." She gave him a stern glance.

"I've always liked vanilla."

"Forget it," she admonished.

He was incredulous. "Forget vanilla ice cream? Never speak to my mother? Give up my car?"

"You know very well what I'm talking about."

"You've been reading too many books. Bachelors can only wish their lives were really what people believe them to be. A bachelor is lonely, forlorn...sad. He needs warm love and good food and a sweet woman to hold." He again tried to take her into his arms.

Resisting, she said, "No, Sam, I've just told you—"

"Come on, baby, cuddle with me. It's cold and icy outside, and I'm a stranger in a strange house with no friends." He grasped her pushing hands, pulling her close enough to nuzzle her throat and the side of her face. He blew gently into her ear and chuckled low in his throat. "Now, then. I've just blown in your ear and you'll follow me anywhere." He released her and walked briskly toward his room, hesitated, looked back, and paused. He frowned at her and sighed in exaggerated irritation. "You're *supposed* to come running after me!"

She shook her head, assuming a serious expression. He examined her face with amused eyes. "There's nothing like a challenge." And feeling no need to explain, he offered his arm formally with a slight bow and said,

"Shall we adjourn to the parlor, Miss Kildaire? I am the champion backgammon player of all northern Indian-apolis—although Gina Stephens tenaciously keeps challenging me for a rematch—and I shall allow you to take lessons for an hour or so. I'll match you a free house call for a simple silk dressing gown."

"That'll be three free house calls to one silk dressing gown!" she objected, as they descended the grand staircase.

"Done. In a deep blood-red."

"Don't count your dressing gown before it's sewn."

"My child, you have no idea what you're up against." He leered at her smugly.

His words could mean many things, and she wasn't sure if he was still talking about backgammon. "Red again," she said. "You're hooked on red."

"Only because you tend to choose it and I like you in that color."

She turned that color too. She'd been making red clothes to wear with him, and she was wearing a red turtleneck with white woolen slacks at that moment. She'd bought the sweater two days ago, and she'd made the slacks yesterday.

Courteously he inquired, "May I bring some friends to your party?"

They were moving the two-seater sofa to face the fire as she asked, "Party?"

He replaced the marble-topped table in front of the sofa and replied, "Yes."

Squatting in front of the cabinet to find the game board, she paused and turned to ask, "The next showing? May's fall showing?"

He looked at her in surprise. "No. St. Patrick's Day."

"St. Patrick's Day?"

"St. Patrick's Day. Anyone named Kildaire would

automatically have a party on St. Patrick's Day. It would be un-American not to."

She couldn't believe that. "Un-American?"

"Of course. Like not having pizza on the Fourth."

"I'm not Catholic."

"Well, you can wear orange! You don't *have* to wear green. Irish Protestants wear orange! But not around the greenies. They tend to get upset."

"What will ever happen to Ireland?" she asked sadly.

"God knows." He shook his head. "And the irony of it all is it's done in the name of God, like in the Middle East. Now don't get me started on that, because we have to talk about the party."

"I haven't had a party since . . . in a long time."

"Then it's time." They shook the dice to see who would lead off, and he won and said that was a portent and he'd choose the silk for his robe during intermission. "How can you say you've had no parties when you have the showings?" he asked.

"That's business," she replied dismissively.

"But they're great parties. With all the big doors slid back into the walls, which opens up the entrance, and the drawing room, the dining room, and this parlor— it's perfect for crowd flow. How many shall we have?"

"We?" she asked cautiously.

"I'll split the cost and bring the booze. Will Hedda cater for a St. Patrick's Day party? We could have a George Washington Carver one to balance."

"We?" she asked again.

"We ought to be able to handle two hundred."

"Two hundred? I don't know that many people."

"I do." Sam counted points, moving his marker. "It'll be a blast. Next year we'll have to screen applicants for invitations."

"Next year?" Things were going too fast.

"Any parrot blood in your family?"

Realizing she'd been repeating his words, she had to ask, "Parrot blood?"

"Right," he said, then added, "You've lost this game. It's your turn, and you can take it if you'd like to go out bloody but unbowed. However, there is no way you can catch up. You could concede and thus practice conceding to me. You'll have a lot of use for the talent. When . . . you marry, will you allow Grendel to be adopted by . . . your husband?"

"If he wants to." She was taking her turn stubbornly.

"You wouldn't mind?"

"If a man loved me enough to marry me, he'd be a man who'd love children, and he'd be a good father to Grendel."

"I have a great many talents besides backgammon." He lowered his eyelids and looked humorously wicked.

She smiled in defeat.

CHAPTER TEN

ICE WAS STILL ticking on the windows when Miss Pru took a new paperback book up to her room to read in bed. Addy and Sam barely interrupted their hotly competitive game to bid her good night. Addy won the second game. Sam said that was only for her morale. He couldn't allow a student to get too discouraged.

"How did you know I liked backgammon?" she asked, curious.

"A glint in the eye, a quickness of the hand, the outthrust of the jaw..." He waved one large hand in small circles as he listed the symptoms.

"You make me sound like a pirate coming on board ship with a cutlass clasped between my teeth."

He nodded and agreed. "Very similar." Then he asked,

"May I have a key to the house?"

That startled her. She said, "A *key?*" as if she hadn't heard him correctly. "I've *told* you, Samuel Grady, that . . ."

He looked at her with tolerant patience and said, "If I'm called on an emergency, I'll need to be able to get back in."

"Oh." That was logical, so she got up and went to the jar in the entrance hall and brought back a key and handed it to him.

Putting it on his key chain, he said, "You wouldn't want me to sleep huddled in the car, freezing to death, not being able to get back inside, would you?"

She frowned. "If you could get back here, you could get back to your own apartment."

"You are the most inhospitable woman! You won't even let me sleep in your room on the floor! You put me clear down the hall in a separate room!"

"You really have no need for that key," she exclaimed and held out her hand. "Give it back."

He smiled.

"Sam."

"The way your lips move when you say my name boggles my mind."

"That's because you're an old roué, a practiced, forty-year-old—"

"Thirty-nine."

"How many years have you been thirty-nine?" She raised supercilious eyebrows.

"Vicious. You won one game and look at you! It's turned you into a smug, predatory, snarling wolverine. I'm terrified." He stretched and yawned. "Tell me about your life and times."

"Are you an old roué?"

"I'm a young, thirty-nine-year-old, innocent boy."

"Hah."

"Now, Addy, you know anyone who's been out in practice five years is still wet behind the ears. I had my nose to the grindstone, studying, from age six to thirty-two. That's almost thirty years! Think about that. I was in school longer than you've been alive."

"What do you know?"

He laughed, then said, "Well . . . a thing or two."

"Can you sew a gusset?"

"It just so happens, madam, that I am quite good at needlework. You should see me do a three-cornered skin tear." He raised his chin and looked down his nose at her. "What would you do with a ruptured intestine?"

"I'd call Marcus. He can fix anything."

Sam frowned at her and said, "So can I." Then, still frowning, he leaned forward. "Come on, I've got to beat you another set to make sure you realize I'm the winner, and then I'll choose the silk for my dressing gown."

She fought to the final roll, but she lost. She gave him a grim, grudging "Good game."

He acknowledged it. "You're an interesting competitor." Then he smiled. "You move so nicely, and when you shake the dice, you jiggle entrancingly—"

"Sam," she began.

"—and I beat you with one hand tied behind my back."

Disgruntled, she said through clenched teeth, "You had the use of both hands."

"No, if you will notice I never moved my left hand off the arm of the sofa."

She looked at his arm and knew he was telling the truth. "Which shows that a one-armed man could play backgammon?"

"Actually, it shows that the skill doesn't involve the use of both hands. It's not like making love. Then you need all four."

"You have four hands?"

"Haven't you ever dated any one of us? We do try to be subtle, but passion brings out all four hands. It's like our third eye."

"Third eye?"

"There's that echo again! The accoustics in this house are remarkable. The third eye is for keyholes. That way your brain is centered as you watch and you're not using only one side—and your nose doesn't get in the way, and your head fits under the doorknob easier."

A chuckle rose inside her as she said, "So you four-armed, three-eyed guys are a bunch of sneaks?"

He nodded gravely. "Would you like to see my third eye?"

She gave him a cautioning look.

"It's in the center of my forehead. It's quite small, so you'll have to look for it very closely. It's small because, of course, keyholes are small; and to look fully you need the entire eye."

Her chuckle escaped and she laughed. "You're really crazy."

He denied that, shaking his head as he explained, "By admitting that we have the third eye, we make people disbelieve us and go undetected." He gave her a small smile and coaxed, "Wouldn't you like to see it?" He reached out his arm and put his hand on the nape of her neck to gently urge her toward him.

"I'm afraid."

His voice went husky and a little rough. "Now why would you ever be afraid of me?"

"It's the threat of the four hands." She suspected that the look of pure innocence she gave him was a little spoiled by the humor she could almost feel dancing in her eyes.

"I'll keep one behind my back," he promised.

"Two," she bargained.

"I'll try," he hedged. Gently he drew her close. She was mesmerized by his mouth. "It's on my forehead," he said. Her eyes moved up to his broad forehead, then caught on his stare, and they smiled at each other before he kissed her.

It was very nice, lying against his sprawled figure, her soft body against his hard one, her mouth being kissed sweetly and his hands moving on her. He used all four. After a time he lifted his mouth and asked, "Did you see it?" His voice was low and intimate and rumbled in his chest.

"What?"

"My third eye."

She shook her head and grinned, amused.

"What did you see?" His hands all moved on her in slow strokings.

"Some comets," she replied lazily. "Colors."

"That's it!"

"Comets and colors?" She was confused.

"I didn't say it was an ordinary eye. When you see it you see comets and colors."

"How nice," she said vaguely. Then she reminded him, "You said you were going to keep two of them behind your back."

"Two of my eyes? How could I?"

"Two of the four hands."

"No, I said I'd *try*. And I did. It was a terrible struggle, but I was distracted from it by some soft, lovely woman who snuggled against me and kept kissing me and running her hands under my sweater."

"I did not!" she protested. "My hands have been right

on your shoulders and along your head the whole time!"

"You're one of *us!* You have four too!"

"Good lord!"

He continued teasing flippantly. "Do you know how our species make love?" His eyelids lowered halfway, and he gave her a scorching glance.

She nodded seriously and replied, "Marvelously."

"Oh, Addy." He buried his face in her throat. "Come to bed with me."

"You promised..."

He lifted his face and frowned into hers. "Whatever made me do a stupid thing like that?"

Her hand went up and smoothed back his hair. "I wouldn't have let you stay if you hadn't promised."

"Let me break it," he coaxed.

"I won't! Just because..."

"Okay, we'll do it your way. I'm willing to wait... No, that's not true. I'm dying for you, but I'll wait until you're ready."

She bit her lip to keep from saying she *was* ready. She tried to sit up, away from him, but he wouldn't have that. "I don't mean to make you uncomfortable," she told him.

"It doesn't make any difference whether you're sitting over there or lying against me. It really doesn't even matter whether I'm *with* you. I want you, Addy. You're never out of my mind. I think I've got a really bad case of you. It's probably fatal." He sighed mournfully.

She kissed his chin, then he brought his mouth to hers, and their kiss was lovely. She sighed and cuddled against him with her head on his chest, and she felt great contentment. She'd never had that particular feeling in her whole life, this comfort she had with Sam, the contentment, the security, the belonging. She looked in the fire and wasn't conscious of any thought but the awareness of him beside her, holding her.

"If . . . you married"—Sam's voice rumbled in his chest—"would you have another child?"

"I hadn't thought about that. I haven't thought about marriage. I doubt any man would marry me. How could he take me home to his mother and say, 'This is Addy. Grendel is her child. She's never—'"

"Not that again! Good lord, Addy, let up! I've never seen anyone who carries such a needless load of guilt. Forgive yourself! *And* what's-his-name. It's *past!*"

But it wasn't past. She'd received that letter.

They talked a long time about all sorts of things, and peace returned to their companionship there by the fire. Sam said he could recognize the pitfalls in raising such a delightful child as Grendel. "It's interesting the casual way you and Miss Pru made her a part of your lives without making a big production of it. It would be easy to overdo with Grendel, since she's so adorable, but you two very carefully trod a narrow path that avoids both the role of seeming indifference and that of ruinous indulgence.

"By your judicious reaction to Grendel's behavior, you can enjoy the range of her personality without having to smother it with discipline or creating a monster child with indulgent delight in her. She's precious anyhow, and her talent of exaggeration is precocious, but what is charming at three can be a pain in the neck at seven.

"You don't make her the center of conversation either, and that has to be almost a miracle. You include her but you don't allow her to interrupt or take over. You're astounding."

"It's mostly Miss Pru," Addy said contentedly. "She's such a lady. How can anyone be tacky around her?"

"And Addy," he added indulgently.

She told him about growing up in that small town,

and all the things she'd done; and he told her stories about his childhood, and they began to know each other as they laughed and sympathized and exclaimed with one another; and they planned the St. Patrick's Day party.

They argued over food until Addy explained that whatever they decided on having, they'd get what Hedda fixed. When the food she made was what you'd asked for, you'd hit an Irish sweepstakes by *guessing* what she'd already planned to serve. And how could you argue with her when she wouldn't speak? But whatever Hedda chose to serve, it would be superb. Sam agreed.

He suggested they just ask people in their age group to this first party and expand it the following year. His words stirred a curious feeling in Addy's stomach. It sounded as if Sam was planning an extended relationship. Addy wondered if she was doomed to be his mistress and knew it would be impossible to refuse. She was only delaying the inevitable. She would eventually be his. She wanted him too badly.

Then she asked herself, Why inevitable? Didn't she have some feeling of self-worth? Why should she settle for a live-in relationship? She was capable of running her own life, and she could step off the track before the train hit her. She could do that. She was a woman, and she was strong. She sat up, straightened her hair with her fingers, and pulled down her red sweater. Red . . . she'd stop wearing red first thing.

They turned out the lights and put the screen in front of the fire before they climbed the grand stairway to the second floor. Addy was braced for the big sales pitch and prepared herself to resist, but Sam only gave her a chaste kiss and wished her a tender good-night.

Pensively she checked Grendel, who was a little warm but sleeping soundly, then went to her room. As she wandered around getting ready for bed, she heard the front door open and close, and footsteps on the stairs. Had he been out already? He couldn't have driven anywhere in that time. He'd already brought in his medical bag. He'd probably been locking up his car.

She wondered if he would come to her room. Her door wasn't locked. If she was smart, she'd get up and lock it, but what if Grendel wakened in the night and came to her locked door? No, she'd just have to take her chances. It surprised her that her mouth smiled and her body stretched like a lazy cat's before she curled up and went to sleep.

She was awakened by a sound in the night. Her first thought was of Grendel. She got out of bed, dragged on her robe, and shoved her bare feet into cold slippers before going down the hall to Grendel's room. She ran into Sam coming out of it and gasped in surprise. He was dressed.

"Where're you going?" she whispered.

He smiled. "I've been and am back. So you really do wear an old flannel bathrobe."

She blushed. Caught in that tacky old thing. Then she recalled saying on the runway, the first time she'd seen him, that she was manless and the robe she was showing wasn't what she wore to bed, and her blush deepened. He'd remembered.

Sam took her down the hall and leaned her against the wall. He opened the robe and put his hands on her warm, flannel-covered body. He held her close to him and put his still-cold nose into the curve of her throat and breathed his hot breath on her skin as he groaned. He kissed her, his hands molding her to the length of him. Then he said, "If you plan to sleep in your own bed, you'd better go now."

She had to pry his hands slowly off her before she could leave him, her eyes caught by his tense, hungry ones, and then he followed her to her door and stood there as she closed it slowly, shutting out his serious stare.

She lay in bed thinking of him with longing. Then the thought intruded: he'd had on different clothes. Where had he gotten them? Had he gone to his apartment and changed? If he could get to his own place, why would he come back here? She knew why. He wanted her. And he had a better chance of getting her if he was in her house.

Then she remembered that just after they'd come upstairs she'd heard him returning from outside. Did he have a suitcase in his car? Was he sneakily moving in? And now he had a house key! And he'd gone somewhere but he'd come back *here*. She sat up, indignant. She would not allow that! She would not! Then her heart picked up its beat. To have him here in the same house? To meet him in the hall in the middle of the night—and have him kiss her with that aching hunger? How long could she hold out against herself?

She put her head in her hands and groaned. Then she thought of when he'd come to her after that little boy had died. He'd been in rumpled clothes and unshaven. Perhaps he carried the kit and clothes in his car. That could be. Then if he needed to stay with a child, he could clean up. That sounded logical. He wasn't moving in on her. He simply carried things with him to use in an emergency. But she wasn't sure...and he had a key to her front door.

What was Miss Pru about, allowing Sam to become a part of the household the way she was doing? Consider tonight, for instance. Sam had dropped in at dinnertime, and both he and Miss Pru had been sure of his welcome. She'd set another place without even asking him if he would like to stay for dinner. Addy narrowed her eyes at the night-darkened ceiling of her room and asked herself, Was Miss Pru matchmaking?

Surely she wouldn't try to bring Addy and Sam together. It would only lead to a broken heart. Sam wanted her. There was no question of that. But he'd never spoken of marriage. He'd asked if *she* had ever gotten married. . . . She couldn't face being abandoned again. Not that she'd missed Paul. But she loved Sam, and if he tired of her and left her . . .

Of course, he had told her he loved her—when he'd made love to her. Love to her—how fantastic it was to be loved by Sam. To be held and to feel his hands and mouth and body on hers. What a stunning thing to be taken by him, to respond, and to be shown the wonders of love with him.

There was a haunting train whistle sounding through the night. Was the train still at a distance, or had it already passed over her? Was she lying wrecked and broken on the tracks? She didn't feel wrecked and broken. Perhaps she still had a chance. How interesting that she wasn't sure.

CHAPTER ELEVEN

WHEN ADDY GOT up the next morning, she set aside the red and white overblouse she'd made and put on a turquoise top over blue-black slacks. She'd show him she wasn't trying to please him. She looked at herself in the mirror as she braided her hair in a single tight braid, and her mirror image looked back with determined confidence and rather high color.

Dressed in a red flannel shirt, plaid pants, and woolly slippers, Grendel had put a stool under her blanket and was sitting cross-legged in front of the resulting tent, arms folded, talking to a row of dolls and animals lined up on her pillows. She looked at Addy cheerfully and invited her to join the row. Addy declined with thanks and felt her daughter's forehead.

From over by the window in the large room, Sam said, "She's fine. A little stuffy, but fine."

Addy turned in surprise and saw Sam, overwhelming one of the small, overstuffed chairs, reading from a stack of journals. "You're up early," she said.

"Early to bed, early to rise, the crafty man gets the prize." He eyed her with appreciation and breathed a soft whistle. "You look fantastic in blue. My God, you could wreck a man's restraint!"

"I thought you liked red!" Addy blurted.

His eyes gleamed. "That was before I saw you in blue."

"Turquoise," she corrected. "Have you eaten?" She had changed the subject from herself, but she felt flustered. Why could he knock her off balance so easily? She straightened her spine and lifted her chin and planted her feet a little more firmly. "Have you had breakfast?"

"Oh, yes. Grendel was lonely and came in."

Addy gasped. "You woke him up?" she asked her daughter.

"He talk in the morning." Grendel spaced the words of her long sentence.

And Sam observed, "Apparently you're not too chatty first light?"

"Are you packed?"

"Well . . . no." He smiled.

"What do you mean, 'No'?" Addy said a little belligerently.

His words permeated with laughter, he chided, "That doesn't sound like the gracious hostess of Ye Olde Inn. You must practice sounding hospitable."

"Sam." Her warning word was sharper, for she'd just realized he was wearing something yet again different: dark blue slacks with a green and blue rugby shirt. Where had they come from?

"Look outside, hostess mine. I believe I'll be around for another day or so."

Her wide eyes opening wider in trepidation, Addy searched his grinning face. Then he rose, took her arm, and led her, faltering, over to the window, where he lifted aside the lace to show her the winter wonderland of an ice-encased world. Every branch, twig, wire, and post was enclosed or covered with ice. The entire landscape was softened with fog.

The silence was the most remarkable thing. There was no traffic coming into the city. She hadn't been aware of that until now. "Listen," she said to Sam. They all stayed silent and listened to the absence of sound.

Companionably, the very large and very small early birds accompanied Addy downstairs and smacked their way avidly through her breakfast. Of course, no one else could show up for the workday, so they declared a holiday. Miss Pru went back to bed. The paperback had been such a good book she hadn't been able to stop reading and had been up very late finishing it.

Addy, Sam, and Grendel checked the birds, who were the only living things moving in that icy world. There was an electric warmer in the birdbath to keep the water from freezing, but they had to throw birdseed on top of the ice; all the rest was frozen underneath it. And since the porches and outside stairs were coated, they had to open windows and pitch the seeds from there. It didn't take long for the birds to find the seed, and they watched them chirping and quarreling and being belligerent. It was incredible to watch those hearty, feathered creatures bathe in the birdbath in that weather.

Sam was woeful. "The sun's due out this afternoon, so it'll all melt pretty fast." When Addy gave him a significant, level look, he chided, "Everyone else is friendly and likes having me around."

She sighed. "But you aren't . . ."

"I aren't what?" he prodded.

"You aren't trying to . . ." And she stopped again.

"Make love to them? What makes you think I'm trying to make love to you?"

Her eyes leaped incredulously to his face, which was so bland and innocent that she became indignant.

He continued to question her in a deadpan way. "Have I made an overt move? Have I kissed you good morning?" Suddenly he grimaced and put his hands to his hair and yelled, *"I've got to have a kiss fix!"* And he lunged at her.

Addy fled, shrieking, and Grendel, squealing, abandoned the birds and got in the way, and Sam swung Grendel up and nuzzled her neck and put her down and went after the fleeing Addy.

Attempting to escape, she ran through the rooms, but then she thought, What are you about, Adelina Mary Rose Kildaire? Men like pursuit! So she stopped and turned, standing straight, and put her hand out in a traffic-cop hand signal.

Not being a motorist, Sam simply ignored her useless gesture and gathered her into his arms and kissed her. Grendel thought that was just hilarious and stomped around and laughed, begging to be next.

Sam had been laughing, but with the kiss his face changed, and he looked at Addy with the sober onslaught of desire. She pulled back. He let her go with great reluctance. His hands lingered on her, threatening to stop their passive release and grab her back. Her fingers escaped last, and she moved away to a safer distance.

Grendel was still squealing and stomping, and without taking his eyes from Addy, Sam picked her up and held her while she wriggled and laughed. He gave the little girl a quick kiss, but his intense gaze never left Addy.

He looked at her from under his brows. He was excessively dangerous for a woman who was wavering in her determination to stay aloof from men. From one man.

With him momentarily distracted from her by the squirming Grendel, Addy turned cautiously and moved away as if from the presence of a wild, threatening beast. She walked carefully so as not to arouse the animal's instinct to pursue.

They were somewhat careful of one another for the rest of the day. Their exchanges were rather formal, as if they sat in a canoe and dared not chance moving and tipping it over. They were stiff and correct. But all in all, it was a marvelous day. Sam's beeper didn't make a sound, the telephone remained silent, and the day was glorious—first in somber, ghostly, foggy, ice-sheathed beauty and later as the magic, crystallized woods sparkled in the sun in awesome glory.

Grendel felt fine. Addy decided that her cold had been minimized by the vitamin C. They spent the day making doughnuts, cautioning Grendel not to eat too many of the "holes" as she did the sugaring. Then they watched an old movie on TV and played hide-and-seek throughout the great house. Addy and Grendel made up the opposition. It was safer that way for Addy. And they read. When Grendel napped, Sam thought he and Addy ought to take a nap too, but she turned her mouth down at the corners and shook her head at him in a reproving way. Unreproved, he grinned at her.

They continued to talk about the St. Patrick's Day party. Addy asked if the models could come. Sam said of course, they were family. She said they couldn't leave out Miss Pru; she loved parties. He agreed and said he knew a fine man who just might do for Miss Pru. She said if they had Miss Pru and the fine man, perhaps they should ask some other people that age. He said he knew a lonely doctor who'd lost his wife just before Christmas, and perhaps a St. Patrick's Day party would be the very thing for him.

Eventually they had almost three hundred people listed. "Sam, do you realize how many people we're supposed to invite?"

"They won't all come," he assured her, waving his hand nonchalantly.

He was wrong. Not only did most of the three hundred people come, but a shocking number also brought friends. Almost everyone who did said, "I *knew* you wouldn't mind."

Everyone trooped in, all in a party mood, and it was a roaring success. Hedda was canny. She apparently knew about St. Patrick's Day parties, because the food did last, but the Irish beer didn't, which would have been fortunate if some happy soul hadn't gone out and come back with a case of Irish whiskey. He denied stoutly that it was from Kentucky. In fact, he threatened to blacken the eye of any black-hearted son who said it wasn't genuine. "It's Irish!" he vowed.

After a judicious sampling, one man declared, "Yeah, I think I can taste it. It's Irish."

Another said, "Do you see any Little People?"

"Not yet."

"'Tis Kentucky," someone claimed.

"Naw, 'tis Irish, pure Irish. Taste that lilt? It's as good as kissing the Blarney stone."

"That work for Germans?" someone asked.

"For anyone with an Irish heart. The outside doesn't count."

The party lasted well into the morning. Addy told Sam, "Your friends certainly have staying power."

"I know. When you think everyone has said good night, you have to watch to be sure they leave. They tend to curl up in corners and sleep until noon, which isn't so bad, but then they want to go on partying."

"You have strange friends," she said, glancing around.

"But they're friendly."

"Yes." Her eyes came back to him. "I noticed the redhead." She gave him a sour look.

"Which one?" He stretched to look over heads.

"They all act that way?"

He gave her a curious, innocent gaze. "What way was that? Show me."

"She couldn't keep her hands off you and was leaning all over you."

"She was just a bit unsteady," he explained in a dismissive way. "High heels do that when you have too much Irish beer. Now you wouldn't for a minute believe that nice girl was being forward."

"She's forward, all right, and every bit of them is silicone!"

Sam threw his head back and laughed. "Come dance with me, my fiery colleen."

"It's too dark and crowded in there." She eyed the unlighted drawing room.

"That's when it's the most fun!" he assured her and led her through the jam of noisy people into the drawing room, where the stereo was playing party music, loud and with a strong beat. Some of it was loud and slow with a strong beat, and required close, slow dancing. Sam held Addy to him, and they swayed and moved against one another, pushed together in the mass of moving bodies. After a time she said, "I don't think we should be dancing. We should be hosting."

"Ummmm" was all he replied. His arms were around her and his hands were at the top of her bottom, pressing her closer and tighter to his hard, muscular frame, to his thighs, to his need of her.

Because his head was down and his mouth was moving on her shoulder, she could whisper in his ear. "You ought not to hold me like this."

"Ummmm. It feels good." He nuzzled her ear and whispered back, "It could feel a whole lot gooder if you'll just come up to my room for a minute or two."

"You don't have a room," she hissed.

"Let's go see if that's right."

"Sam! Cut that out!"

"I think it was that guy in back of you."

"It was *you!*"

"Now, you know I'd never do anything like that," he purred.

"Then how do you know what I'm talking about?"

And he laughed.

It was hot in the room with all those bodies moving and swaying and rubbing together. He kissed her, and she became a little faint. She thought that must be because the room's oxygen was all used up by that mass of people. After a few more kisses, she was almost ready to help him find out if he did have a room after all. That was when an orange-shirted man took umbrage over something a green-tied man said and suggested that his face was put together wrong and volunteered to rearrange it.

Their argument gathered a knot of pleasantly interested onlookers whose heads turned in tennis-tournament fashion as the insults became more intricate. When the opponents' faces became a little red and their words somewhat harsher, someone stopped the stereo and began to play "When Irish Eyes Are Smiling" on the piano. The song was taken up readily by the crowd and diverted most of the witnesses to the altercation. After that came "Mother Machree." What pseudo Son of the Old Sod

could quarrel during "Mother Machree," Addy thought.
It would be un-American.

When Grendel came down for a brief peek at the party,
wearing her long brown flannel nightgown with a matching peaked nightcap, two people swore off Irish whiskey.
An Irish-whiskey ex-doubter laid one finger to the side
of his blunt nose and vowed, "I see 'em."

The recipient of that confidence scoffed, "Naw, 'tis
moonshine."

"'Tis Irish whiskey," the new believer proclaimed.

"What Irish whiskey?" chimed in a disbeliever. "It's
straight from Nashville! That's where this whiskey comes
from. Hear the music?"

"That's from the piano," came a sober contribution.

"You don't say!"

"Cut it out, you guys," interjected a third party.

With dignity he was told, "We're having a—spir-
ited—discussion," which brought hilarious laughter for
the clever wording.

Linda, the brunette model, showed how to go-go dance
and gathered an intent following and some imitators.
Jeremy Tinker, Sam's friend and Grendel's doctor, flirted
with all the women but was carefully formal with Addy,
whom he referred to as Sam's girl.

When Addy met Diana Hunter's husband, she hid her
surprise nicely. So Diana was safely married and could
have no interest in Sam. Diana told Addy that Sam looked
great but a little frazzled. "What are you doing to him,
Addy?" she asked.

"Nothing."

Diana laughed. "He's in love with you."

"How can you tell?"

"He can't keep away from you. He has his hands or
eyes on you all the time."

"That's just . . . well . . . he wants . . ."

"Sex? That too. He's never been like this with any other woman he's ever dated. He's been polite and humorous and fun, but he's never been the way he is with you. When are you going to put him out of his misery?"

"I don't want to get involved with any man."

Diana hooted. "Yeah. Sure. You're totally uninvolved!" And she laughed immoderately.

Besides the dancers, the arguers, and the serious drinkers, there were couples draped together on the stairs, against walls, on piled-up furniture, and in hidden corners. All in all it was a landmark party, and everyone had a hell of a good time.

When Sam said just that to Addy, she said pointedly, "A 'hell' of a good time?"

"They're having a good time now. Tomorrow will be hell. Headaches, upset stomachs, being tired...Only they won't remember that. They'll only remember the fun."

When they eased the last of the guests out of the house, it was almost five. The birds were starting to chirp. Alone at last, Sam and Addy gave each other weary smiles. "Whose idea was this party?" Addy wanted to know.

Sam denied any part of it. "*My* name's not Kildaire!"

"Isn't Grady an Irish name?"

"I think after tonight it'll have to be."

"Tonight was a christening of the non-Irish?"

"I'm sure of it." He nodded profoundly. "Just wait. Next February everyone who was here tonight will start saying, 'Faith, now, we'll be having our party on our day, right?'"

"It's monstrous."

He nodded gravely. "In three years we'll have to hire a hall. We'll have outgrown the house."

"We'll have..." And she stopped. "We" sounded

extremely linked. Sam and she were becoming a "we." She mustn't let that happen.

She resisted his good-night kiss in the entrance hall. She said she had to look around for burning cigarettes, and told him to go on. She went through the rooms and the kitchen, emptying the last of the cigarette stubs into the tin box there.

When she went wearily upstairs, she was startled to see Sam coming out of the bathroom, in a toweling robe that was his. He paused and smiled at her. "Want me to bathe you? I know you're tired, and you'll sleep better if you relax first with a nice bath. I'll help you, and that will hurry you into bed."

Sure he would. "No. What are you doing here?"

"I'm going to crawl into bed and, being newly Irish, I must have a personal leprechaun for a guardian angel. And I'll pray my leprechaun delivers you to me." His voice and face were serious and watchful.

She shook her head, and her eyes fell before his. She had to swallow and stiffen her backbone before she could say a reasonably steady good-night.

She stepped into the shower and found herself faced with the truth. He was spending the night. No ice or snow or sickness. They'd given a party, and he was spending the night. Why hadn't she told him to run along home? He'd just assumed he would be welcome. And he'd stayed. He couldn't do that. She yawned, so sleepy she couldn't argue with any force at the moment. She'd have to tell him about it in the morning...when they wakened later that day. He really couldn't do that. He had his own apartment and he could go on home just like everyone else. When had he brought that robe into the house? She dried herself and drooped into her room— and there he was, in her bed! He was asleep.

He was truly asleep, snoring a nice, purring snore and out cold. He was sleeping so soundly that she was tempted to climb into bed. When he wakened, she'd say, "You were fabulous," just to see his face as he tried to remember making love to her. That would be funny. The only reason she didn't do that was that she couldn't figure out a way to escape the bed if he did wake up and find her there. What if she didn't want to escape?

She toyed briefly with the idea of getting into *his* bed. He'd said he was going to see if his personal leprechaun would put her there. But again, after the joke was over, how would she get away?

So she went to bed in the room beyond Grendel's. But she dreamed of Sam the whole night long, wild erotic dreams of frustration and need. It was an exhausting sleep.

CHAPTER TWELVE

SAM WAS GRUMPY the next day. He didn't come downstairs until afternoon. He stumped around the kitchen making his breakfast as if he were at home. Addy smiled slyly at him. "What's so funny?" he wanted to know.

"Your leprechaun put me in your bed, and you never did show up!" But she couldn't control her humor.

"Yeah. Sure." His tone was disbelieving.

She looked innocent. "Where *ever* were you? I went to sleep waiting." And she sighed a long, gusty sigh. But she was making a mistake.

He got up and went to her and grabbed her hand as she turned in belated alarm to flee. He jerked her back and held her against him. "It isn't a subject for teasing me, Addy. I love you and I want you like blue murder. I'm being very civilized about your hesitation—"

"Hesitation!"

"Yes. I'm going to get you, and the sooner you realize it the better for both of us." Then he kissed her until she was boneless. He did that deliberately, knowing what he was doing to her, she was sure, and when he'd made her realize that she wanted him just as terribly, he released her, put her from him, and sat down and ate his breakfast with every appearance of being calm.

She stood there, a shambles, and looked around the kitchen in a daze, not quite knowing what to say or do, but not wanting to walk out of the room. If she left, it would seem as if she was running away. It would be cowardly.

"Do you have a headache?" Sam asked conversationally.

"No."

"I have a bearcat."

"Take two aspirin."

He smiled. "Yes, Doctor."

"I don't have to have a medical degree to know to take two aspirin for a hangover."

He denied that. "I don't have a hangover. It's just a headache. All that cigarette smoke and all the frustration gave me a tension headache."

"Two aspirin," she advised again.

"I know a better way."

"Yes, I know. You want to tumble me and get rid of your headache, but you'd just give it to me. You'd give me all the problems, when I don't need any more problems."

"You wouldn't get pregnant," he assured her gently.

"And that makes it okay? A nice friendly tumble to rid you of your frustrations? No involvement, no...*side* effects? Having sex isn't that casual for me."

"It isn't casual for me either. And, Addy, I don't just want sex. I want love."

"Exclusive rights, you mean. Live-in convenience. 'Hey, I've got a headache! Come on, hurry up, hop in bed!' No, thanks."

"Hard-hearted Hannah," he accused.

"Blame me. That's typically male. Go yowl under some other woman's window."

"Like Tippy's?" He slid a cool glance at her.

"Tippy?" She gave him a still look in return.

"The redhead who was leaning on me," he elaborated.

"Her name's Tippy? How appropriate! She looks round-heeled."

"Why, Addy! What a catty thing to say. If I didn't know better, I'd think you were jealous."

"I am not!"

"Of course not," he agreed smugly. "Could I have another piece of toast?"

Automatically she took a piece of bread from the wrapper and slid it into the toaster while he watched her, his eyes gleaming. They were silent for a while. When the toast popped up, Addy buttered it and gave it to him, and nodded once to his thanks. Her eyes followed his movements as he put jam on the toast and then bit into it. Then she said, "She wouldn't have to worry about getting her hair mussed up. It's a mess anyway."

"Whose hair?"

"Tippy's."

"I think her hair's not messy so much as . . . casual."

"Probably can't get a comb through it. I'll bet no man's ever managed to kiss her."

"You mean you think she's . . . pure?" That obviously surprised him.

"Naw, I mean she puts her lipstick on so thick that

anybody trying to kiss her would slide right off her mouth."

Sam laughed immoderately and choked on the toast, and Addy had to pound his back, which she did with great goodwill.

They were still being a little formal when he left after supper. Grendel couldn't understand why he had to leave, why he couldn't just stay there. He told Grendel her mother was inhospitable. Grendel wasn't sure what that meant, but she gave Addy a censuring look, until Sam picked her up and kissed her and told her to behave and mind her mother, that he'd be back. He kissed Addy too, but he only leaned down and gave her a peck.

The days passed, and Sam was there more than anywhere else, but he didn't stay overnight again. He mentioned it, but Addy didn't allow it, and she didn't make up the bed under the coverlet.

Sam brought her candy, flowers, books, and gloves. With the fifth pair of gloves she told him that was enough. He said with asperity that giving presents was what courting men did and she'd have to put up with it.

"Sam, I've told and *told* you I don't want to get involved with you!" And she went on at great length repeating her reasons.

"I don't see how you think you still have the choice."

"I mean it, Sam."

But when he didn't come by one day, she called and asked if he was all right. "No, I'm not!" he replied glumly.

"What's wrong? Are you ill?" She was alarmed.

"You bloody well ought to know what's the matter with me."

"Oh, Sam . . ."

Gradually Addy forgot about Paul Morris's letter, filed under "M," which had inquired whether Grendel was his daughter. She didn't reply to it, and she assiduously didn't think about it or Paul. She mostly just thought about Sam.

Marcus told Addy he'd found Emmaline a little abandoned shop that was exactly what she needed. They all went to inspect it and consider it critically, but it really was just right. They went each day as Marcus's crew cleaned it up, and Emmaline chose the paint. Addy listened to her specify the rather startling color combination and waited for Marcus to object. He didn't, which made Addy indignant. When she got him away from Emmaline, she asked, "Why does Emmaline get to choose her colors? I wanted my house white and you didn't paint it white, you painted it blue. How come?"

Patiently, Marcus told her, "Just wait. She's exactly right. It'll be perfect."

And it was. It was eye-catching, a little wild, but it was instantly apparent that the store held unusual, high-quality, stunning goods. And it did. She named it Emmaline's, and they made a ceremony when the sign went up. It amazed Addy to observe Emmaline's slow laziness turn into élan, to see her movements take on confidence, to watch her become a stern taskmaster.

Emmaline had hired two young people. Addy met them, found them talented and cheerful, and liked them both. Marcus found two young men to help her. One maintained the books and kept track of the orders, and the other was the salesman. Both were businesslike, clear-eyed, and competent. Emmaline made them all toe the line.

"Emmaline is turning into a tyrant!" Addy told Marcus.

"She'll mellow after she's used to being boss," he soothed.

"I think we've got a black, female Hitler on our hands."

"Go wash out your mouth with soap."

Just before the middle of April a great storm threatened. Addy had been watching its approach. As tree limbs were tossed and the husks of dead leaves were strewn across the yard, she saw Sam's car turn into her driveway. She ran to the front door to let him in.

"Hurry!" she called, flinching under the onslaught of blustering winds buffeting her, plastering her clothes to her body and streaming through her hair.

He ran up on the porch, and together they looked at the inky sky to the southwest. The morning sun gave a last sweep of light, spotlighting the young, tender green leaves against the slate-black sky. The colors were breathtaking.

They pushed the door closed and stood smiling at each other as Addy combed her hair with her fingers. "The radio said severe weather and a tornado watch," Sam said, "so I came right over."

Grendel came to the landing of the grand staircase and yelled, "You're *here!*" in a most charming welcome.

"Come see what I have for you," Sam invited.

"What?" She came down the stairs one at a time, sliding her hand along the railing.

Sam held an Irish, crushable hat in one big hand. As Grendel reached the bottom of the stairs, he squatted down and held the hat low so she could see into it. He'd brought her a kitten. It was mostly ears and eyes, with an enormous purr. Addy cautioned Grendel that it was a baby cat and must be carefully held so as not to be hurt. Grendel was enchanted and watched it, amazed. Sam put it on the rug, and its eyes got bigger and its short tail stood straight up. Grendel laughed.

"Be careful of it," Addy repeated.

"She will," Sam said.

The kitten, young as it was, knew to get under the sofa or some inaccessible place when it needed to rest. And Grendel's wrists soon showed light scratches. The kitten was teaching her what was permissible. They named it Stormy to honor the day.

They played with the kitten until it had had enough and retreated under the back of a large, low sofa in the drawing room. Grendel wailed because she couldn't get to it.

"Let's play hide-and-seek or hare and hounds," Sam suggested.

"You're it!" Addy proclaimed.

The house was made for hare and hounds. Sam would almost catch Addy, but she'd reverse or dodge aside and he'd allow it. In the meantime, Grendel would flee and squeal and get in the way deliberately to get caught and kissed on the cheek and then released while Addy ran free.

After a time Grendel became tired and bored, and Sam set her up with books and the kitten in her room. Then he went back downstairs, and the game took on a different tone as he chased Addy silently. It was no longer hare and hound. It was more like cat and silent, skittering mouse.

Eventually Addy was trapped in the morning room and couldn't get out. She retreated, breathless and laughing, stepping backward, her hands up, seeking an escape and finding none. Sam advanced slowly, silently, relentlessly, his lips parted slightly to accommodate his quickened breath. His eyes were intense and serious.

"I give up," Addy said, then, at his inflamed look, she quickly changed it to "King's X" and crossed her fingers on both hands, still backing away from him. The only door available led to a huge closet they used for storage. Prolonging her freedom, she opened the door, darted inside, and closed it, holding the knob. It was dark in there, but it was refuge.

But the door opened outward, and there was no way she could hold out against him. He simply turned the knob and pulled it open. He stood in the doorway and looked at her trapped inside the closet. Then he stepped inside too, clasped her arm as he closed the door, and was there in the dark with her. His other arm swept around her to pull her strongly against him as he bent his head, searching in the dark for her mouth.

She gasped, whispering, "Sam..." in almost a plea.

"Oh, Addy," he groaned, and there was no quarter in his voice. Her mouth trembled under his fiercely demanding kiss, and she uttered little sounds as her hands fluttered around his head, her body pressed tightly against his.

His hands shook as they moved on her, molding her body. While her breath seemed caught in her throat, his was warm and close as he tugged her blouse over her head and unhooked her bra. He growled very low, "Undo your hair and *never* wear it braided like that again."

Without arguing, she fumbled to obey him. He took advantage of her body while her arms were up to her hair. When her hair was freed, he almost paused as he ran his hands gently through it, cupping her head and putting his face into the silken mass. Then he jerked off his sweat shirt and stood with his hands on her sides. He tugged her to him until her nipples touched his chest, and his palms slid up to cup the sides of her breasts, pressing them together so that the soft mounds pushed against his hairy chest.

She was becoming boneless and had to lean against him to remain erect. She heard him gasp. Her head was too heavy to hold up and it fell back; one of his hands supported its weight as he kissed her. Their mouths melded in a scorching embrace, and their bodies rubbed against each other, each of them relishing the feel of the other as they clung together in the dark closet.

There could be no denying his need of her. Hers for him was not so obvious, for she wasn't skilled or practiced. She was so amazed by the sensual thrills flooding her that her mind was turned inward, swamped by self-absorption, with no thought of giving him pleasure.

She was only able to receive sensations from him, and she did, all kinds of sensations—wild, lovely, and thrilling. She moved and squirmed and wriggled and gasped and began to reach for him to fill the growing need to hold and touch him. She was so filled with passion that she wasn't aware of how much bolder she'd become, and how she thrilled him in turn. It was inadvertent; she was concentrating on her own sensations.

Almost desperate, he laid her on the dark closet floor and allowed his tense, sweaty body to seek brief relief as he quickly took her. She moaned in disappointment as he lifted from her, but he didn't release her. He laid her back down again and began to make love to her. He showed Addy that it wasn't only sexual satisfaction he desired from her. It was her love.

He played her body like a virtuoso, and they both took pleasure in his skill. They shared the dark closet for a long time that stormy morning as he taught her many things about herself and about him. She was an impetuous student, and he had to restrain her before she learned to take her time. And in their paradise, she heard the sound of a train whistle roaring over her head as it rushed on past. She smiled in the dark and kissed him again softly, her tongue touching his lips. Then, as his penetrated into her mouth, she gently sucked it and moved under him and thought how lovely it was to walk on tracks of love. Why had she been afraid?

She put her arms around him and hugged him down to her. She moved her face over his and kissed along his shoulder and murmured to him. She heard his voice ask urgently, "Did you say you loved me?" She paused and was still, lying there naked on the closet floor with her love fused to her, and she nodded slowly. "You love me?" his harsh whisper demanded again.

In a tiny voice, she admitted, "Yes."

"Ahhhhh." He relaxed on her and made an almost purring sound into the side of her throat. "Tell me," he urged. "Let me hear you say it."

"I . . . love you." Her voice sounded uncertain and faint. Her last defenses were down. He would move in, and she'd become his mistress.

"Oh, my love," he breathed passionately, "I love you." His hands cradled her head, and he kissed her so sweetly that tears came to her eyes. He tasted them. "Tears? Honey?" And he kissed her face and her eyes and murmured of his love and his happiness that she loved him. And he said his life was complete.

Then he moved on her, coaxing her again to follow him in his desire, and he built their pleasure until they rode along the peak, balancing on the edge, hesitating, allowing it to falter, then to build again until they swept over it into that glorious explosion and on into thrilling, falling sensations. Still, it left a core of hunger in Addy that she was again eager to fill.

Later they lay for some time, limp and surfeited. "I've never before enjoyed hide-and-seek quite so much," Sam said. "I hadn't known it could be so much fun."

Addy groaned. "I imagine it will be days before I'll be able to walk."

He comforted her. "Being a doctor, I know of treatments to help you."

"I suspect exactly what you have in that busy little mind."

He laughed, filled with himself and his love for her.

He couldn't keep his hands off her, but now they were gentle and caressing. He kissed her a great deal, and she lay lax and submissive. When she asked what time it was, he put his arm near the bottom of the door so he could see his watch. It was almost noon.

Addy was appalled. "We have to get dressed right this minute and get lunch for Grendel!"

But he was in no hurry. "I'll always love rainstorms for the rest of my life."

"You're an opportunist."

"I am not either! I'm a serious lover!"

"I can vouch for that. You're fantastic!"

"Do you really think so?"

She nodded, so he had to kiss her again, and she was on her back again. "Behave!" she scolded.

"I can't possibly make love to you again, but I certainly enjoy seeing you in that position and naked."

Disbelieving, she asked, "How can you see me in the dark?"

"I'm part cat, if you recall, so I can look at your loveliness."

"You're a voyeur?"

"Oh, no. I'd never only want to look. I'm committed to total involvement."

They finally opened the door a crack so they could see to get dressed. They combed their hair with their fingers and smiled at each other foolishly. They held hands and whispered to each other as they left the closet and squinted at the sunshine that flooded from the study into the wide back hall. They stood there and laughed at each other, and Addy felt herself blushing a little, so Sam had to lean over and kiss her yet again. Then he had to put an arm around her, and they went through the back hall into the kitchen.

Of course, they were sure they looked perfectly ordinary, but Miss Pru gave them a brief, weighing glance, then shook her head. But she was smiling. Sam kissed her cheek. Then he leaned down and kissed Grendel, who jabbered about the doll Miss Pru had made for her from all sorts of scraps of material. She held it up so they could see that the doll's "flesh" was a crazy quilt and quite charming. Grendel was trying to decide on a name for it.

The lovers leaned against the counter close together, their arms loosely around each other. Addy had tried twice to move away from Sam's side, but he wouldn't have it. He yawned and yawned and grinned.

Miss Pru gave them soup and sandwiches, which they neglected. They took desultory bites as they smiled at each other and at Grendel. Finally Miss Pru insisted that they eat, and they obediently finished their sandwiches.

Miss Pru bustled around straightening up the kitchen, and Grendel said she had to have her nap and asked her dolly if she was sleepy. In a low voice Sam asked Addy if she was sleepy, and his eyes were filled with lazy laughter. They trailed Grendel and Miss Pru up the stairs and watched them disappear into Grendel's room. They were still in the hallway—and kissing—when Miss Pru went by on her way to her own room. She trailed a hand along their shoulders and said, "Nap-nappy."

They turned to watch her go down the hall, but she didn't look back, and then they were alone. Addy smiled and repeated, "Nap-nappy," as she touched Sam's face. She turned from him to go to her room, and he simply followed. She hesitated, watching him. He grinned and began quite naturally to take off his clothes. She continued to watch, admiring his muscular, powerful body as it was unsheathed. He came over to her, took off her clothes—more leisurely this time—and stood back to look down at her. He gave a shake of his head and said, "Gorgeous." Then he led her to the bathroom, and they showered and dried each other, taking a long time with each other's bodies, taking pleasure in having their hands on each other.

They went back to Addy's room and crawled into her bed. They wound their arms around each other, sighed in contentment, and fell asleep.

They didn't waken until late afternoon. Sam wanted her again, and his kisses were earnest and his hands urgent. Addy protested that he couldn't possibly! But he insisted that yes he could, she had no idea how long he'd dreamed of her, of having her in bed with him and making love with her.

Ever since he'd seen her up on that runway showing that robe... "Oh, by the way, I have something for you." He tugged her out of bed and down the hall to "his" room, and there in the closet she gasped to see two suits and three shirts!

She said, "What...?" She'd stripped the bed after the St. Patrick's Day party but hadn't checked the closet.

He reached in and took a box from the shelf. It was a Gown House box. "Here," he said to her, "I bought this for you."

She was surprised and frowned a little as she took the box over to the bed, opened it, and... it was the robe she'd modeled. She couldn't believe it. She took it out and looked at it, then turned to Sam.

He was smiling smugly, his hands on his bare hips, his interest rising. "Model it for me...so I can undo that third hook."

She continued to look at him, and her grin couldn't stay hidden. "Was it really for me?"

"I was afraid you'd sell it, and I wanted it for you so I could be the only one to see you in it and undo those hooks."

"That day, you looked as if you were going to bid on *me*."

"I can see why you thought so. I felt the same way."

"And you got me." Was her tone a bit rueful?

"I finally did," he agreed.

"That other time...you had me then too," she reminded him.

"That was more compassion on your part, and it was beautiful, but I wanted you to make love with me because you wanted me, not just to comfort me."

"Oh? I had a choice this morning?"

"After the first several times." He grinned at her. "I had to be sure you realized how it was with me so you'd finally be eager and willing."

"You're terrific. I had no idea it could be that way."

"Truthfully, neither did I."

"I love you, Sam."

"Come here."

"You're incredible."

"You should wait and try me when I don't have to be restrained." He looked excessively sassy.

"You're restrained?"

"Killingly."

She hooted, disbelieving, but it wasn't long before she believed. He put her down on the bed and tumbled her around and tousled her hair and squeezed and patted and kissed and mouthed her. She was astounded when he aroused her to fever pitch, and then he made her work to convince him, but he was a pushover.

He stayed for supper as naturally as if he'd lived there all along. He and Grendel set the table and chatted. But the kitten was very distracting for Grendel, and she had to keep checking on where it was. Sam chided her that when she had a job to do, she should finish it before she went on to something else. And Addy listened and thought what a good influence Sam would be on her daughter. The thought of Grendel's real father, off in the shadowy distance, tried to intrude, but Addy pushed it aside.

After Grendel and Miss Pru went upstairs, Sam and Addy sat talking. When it came time to go to bed, Sam delayed. Addy was very sleepy. "Aren't you ready to come upstairs?" she asked.

He turned his mouth down at the corners and did a lousy imitation of Addy when she had said, "I'm not a 'convenient lay' just because *you* need sex and haven't any control."

"Oh, be quiet!" Addy said. She reached out for his sleeve and pulled him up the stairs.

He feigned a great struggle—not disturbing her progress or the sleeve she held—then sighed elaborately in surrender, and in a terrible try for a high voice, he grieved, "I'll probably hate myself in the morning."

"You're perfectly safe," Addy assured him.

They debated which room they'd share. He said, "Since it's your house, I'd look like a gigolo if I crawled into your bed. It would seem more hospitable and gracious if you'd come to me."

That made her smile and, shaking her head, she went to his room. They had to make up the bed. He wanted to bathe her again, but she said, "Forget it. You're too tired, and I'd just get all excited and demand you submit and you'd cry, and I'd feel like a rat for forcing you."

"I don't think I'm that tired."

"Well, I am. You're just like a little boy with a new toy, and you should put me down and go to sleep."

"This isn't turning out quite as I'd planned."

She snored ostentatiously.

"I think a convenient headache is more ladylike than snoring," he said.

She didn't reply. He took her carefully in his arms and settled down. They were quiet for a while, then she whispered, "Aren't you glad I didn't want to?"

"You're a wretch and shut up." But he laughed, genuinely amused.

CHAPTER THIRTEEN

THEY WAKENED EARLY and grinned at each other before Sam asked, "You won't be stubborn and arbitrary and have to be married in June, will you?"

"Married?" she asked cautiously.

"Yeah."

"You want...to marry me?"

"What in hell did you think all this courting was all about? All those gloves and risking you getting pimples from all that candy..."

"Me?" She was a little breathless.

"You are Adelina Mary Rose Kildaire, aren't you?" She nodded.

"Then you're the one," he assured her. "I want to share the rest of my life with you." He lay on his side, smiling at her, then he became serious. "You're just gorgeous, lying naked in bed with your hair all messed up."

In something of a daze, she responded, "I'm all covered up, and you can't possibly see me."

"I have hands, honey, and I can feel, and you're just gorgeous."

"Sam? Do you really want to marry me?"

Very seriously he replied, "I honest to God thought you realized that."

"I just thought you wanted to get me in bed."

"Oh, you were certainly right about that! But I want exclusive rights for the rest of my life."

"You make it sound as if I'd be sleeping around if we weren't married."

"The exclusive rights include all the rest—your debts, your comfort, your protection, your cherishing. All those things too. Sex is one of the perks."

"Oh, Sam, I would love to be married to you." She flung herself at him, and their kiss quickly became ardent.

He pulled away from her a bit. "Are you just after my fabulous body?" He frowned at her suspiciously.

"So I get that too?"

And he had to show her that she did.

When they went down to breakfast, Addy had on a fiery-red sweater with red-and-black-plaid slacks, and her hair was loose around her shoulders. And her smile was tender and dewy.

Miss Pru exclaimed elaborately at their announcement and made them laugh. Addy figured that was where Grendel got her dramatics. Grendel looked intrigued by it all, though not quite clear as to what it all meant, but she exclaimed in echo to Miss Pru's comments.

Sam picked Grendel up and said he'd like it very much

if she'd call him Daddy. She tried that out and thought it sounded funny. But Sam kept coaxing her to call him Daddy.

Miss Pru opened a bottle of champagne, and they toasted the future and each other during breakfast and decided April fifteenth would be The Day. There was no need to wait. All the designs for the May show were finished, and almost all were sewn and fitted. Miss Pru could handle any other fittings. Sam and Addy could have a three-day honeymoon before they had to return to complete the line garments and for Addy to learn the narration for the fall showing the first of May.

Addy designed her wedding gown and took the material to Emmaline, who put a border of wild flowers around the bottom of the skirt in a riot of color. It was stunning.

Addy and Grendel took Sam to meet her parents, and they all survived it. Eyeing her cousins, one two years old and the other almost one, Grendel was very quiet. The kitten, Stormy, had had to stay in Indianapolis, and Addy knew Grendel was anxious to get back to it.

Addy's next younger sister was married and pregnant with her third child. Without being asked, she said she wouldn't be able to be Addy's attendant, since she was so pregnant. Then she fidgeted impatiently and finally asked, "Are you getting married because you're pregnant . . . again?"

Addy was stunned. So her family had speculated that she was pregnant again and that at least this time she'd get married! She said a stiff, "No."

Her sister went to the door of the living room and called, "Mama!" When she had their mother's attention, she shook her head in an exaggerated way.

They shocked Addy, and she was glad to leave.

* * *

Sam still slept at Addy's—and with her—before their marriage. One day, as he was bidding Addy good-bye prior to leaving for the hospital, he leaned over to give her a kiss, and Grendel hopped around, asking for a kiss too. A woman who was there to choose a gown laughed and said it was easy to see who was Grendel's daddy.

Grendel replied carefully, in her version of English, "April fifteenth. That's when Sam's my daddy. He and Mommy exercise, and I hear them."

The woman gave an audible gasp, flustered. Sam's dancing eyes watched Addy blush before he put in smoothly, "Aerobics." He smiled at the woman, whose turn it was to blush. Sam couldn't resist asking, "Whatever were you thinking?" and he tsked as he left, shaking his head.

Marcus's gang mended the porch for the wedding. With the weather uncertain, it might well be nice enough for the guests to sit on the porch. Addy watched them working and asked Marcus, "That wood isn't new. Where did you get it?"

Not really paying any attention to her, Marcus replied, "We tore down a house."

Addy stared at him. "Just to get wood for this porch? Did they catch you?"

Marcus turned to her and laughed out loud. "The house was due to be demolished, and we got the job. We did it by hand instead of the wrecking ball. We sell the windows, kindling, and bricks. It gives the young men something to do and a little cash. You knew that, Addy."

She looked at the planks, embarrassed. She hadn't actually accused Marcus, but she felt uncomfortable. The planks saved her. "How do I know you aren't bringing me three nests of termites?"

"Trust me."

Her eyes came up to his, and she grinned. They understood each other. Impishly she asked, "Do you know what Emmaline is charging me for her work?"

His eyes danced as he suggested, "By the piece?"

Since that was how she'd paid the slow Emmaline for sewing, she had to laugh too. "She has to be kin to you, Marcus, she's so heartless in her prices."

"She's worth it."

"I know, I know. And so are you."

"Hedda has your eats planned for the hitching. You gonna jump over a broom?"

"That's what does it? Jumping over a broom makes it legal? If that does it, why all the fuss?"

"Pearl showed me your dress—that Emmaline did."

"She did the flowers! I couldn't wait long enough for her to sew it too! I'd never get married! You coming to watch?"

"Oh, yes."

"You're really coming just to eat," Addy declared. "You don't fool me at all."

"That too. My Hedda's a supreme cook."

"Why aren't you fat?" she asked with interest.

"It isn't what she cooks as the way she does it. It all tastes so good I never realize she makes me diet."

"Does she speak to you?" Addy wanted to know.

"In many ways," he replied. Then he said, "Your Sam is a good man."

It wasn't until later, when Addy thought about it, that she realized Marcus hadn't really told her if Hedda could speak or if she simply chose not to. They were an interesting, talented pair. Finally, as she thought about them, the puzzle of Marcus suddenly fell into place. She told Sam, "Marcus is a mechanical engineer and does consulting."

Sam said, "Umm-hmm."

"How did you know?"

"You mean you just guessed?"

"That explains his absences. He's helping someone else for a change." She grinned as she gave her head a shake. "I tried to set him up in business in a repair shop in my basement." And Sam laughed with her.

The day of the wedding Hedda came up the stairs in her slow, stately way and entered the room where Addy was dressing. Addy smiled at her and was rewarded with one of Hedda's rare, marvelous smiles. Then Hedda gave a regal nod of her head and handed her a small pouch. She indicated it was to be pinned to her bra between her breasts.

Addy took it cautiously and felt it crackle delicately. Voodoo. Some sort of African witchery, that's what it was. Sam would inhale it and it would act as an aphrodisiac. She glanced at Hedda respectfully but a little fearfully. Hedda touched the red roses Addy would carry and then the small pouch. It was rose petals. Hedda gave her an extremely amused, slanting glance and left the room.

So Sam and Addy were married. Addy's mother and father both cried. Addy figured it was for joy that she was no longer an unwed mother. Sam's mother and stepfather and various relatives were courteous and pleasant to Addy's rather stiff family. They were all witness to a brief adoption ceremony that made Sam Grendel's father.

They were drinking toasts when the first of the unexpected guests arrived. Only Hedda, who had shrewdly witnessed the St. Patrick's Day party, didn't look surprised. Eventually more than two hundred people tramped in, bringing their own drinks and all sorts of gifts, but mostly plants. They were dressed in all manner of styles, all were in a party mood, and they settled down to celebrate.

The crowd glanced up and cheered when Addy and Sam came down the grand staircase and went out the front door to Sam's car. Addy wore her red going-away suit. But their leaving would be only a brief interruption, they knew, and wasn't enough to disturb the course of the party.

Driving away in the car, Addy wanted to know, "Why are we leaving so soon? The party is just getting started."

"Your sister told Jeremy that Hedda gave you a voodoo pouch with an aphrodisiac that'll drive me wild."

"It's just dried rose petals sewn into a little pouch so I'll smell nice," Addy said deprecatingly, with the wordly tolerance of a sophisticate for a small-town friend.

But Sam was certain. "It has to be an aphrodisiac because I'm affected. I can tell."

"Oh, silly, you're always that way."

"This is worse," he insisted.

"*Worse?*" she exclaimed incredulously.

He tried for a more accurate word. "Better?"

"Will you still want to make love with me now that it's legal?"

"Yes." He was positive about that too.

"Will you like it as well? Since it's no longer forbidden fruit?"

"I'll let you know," he promised in a way that showed he knew scientific research was vital.

"If we have a baby right away, we could get one in before you turn forty."

"I already have a daughter," he told her contentedly.

"You do?" She turned wide eyes to him.

"Grendel. We signed the papers just a while ago."

"Oh."

"Did you think . . . ?"

"Well..." She faltered.

"I've told you everything important that's happened to me," Sam declared sternly.

"No, you haven't! You haven't told me one single thing!"

"That's the reason. Nothing important happened to me until I met you."

Their honeymoon was the way honeymoons are supposed to be—laughter, remembering when each was attracted to the other, how they felt, what they'd thought, interspaced with lots of loving and catching up on sleep.

Lying naked on her stomach, examining Sam's face as he lay partially under her, Addy said, "I wonder if I'll ever get used to looking at you."

"Oh, sure. Pretty soon my face will be as familiar to you as your own."

"Uh... *my* face doesn't give me erotic feelings."

"That's strange! Your face affects *me* that way!"

It was momentous only to them. They finally returned to the big house on the north side of Indianapolis and to Grendel, who whooped and called Sam Daddy nearly every other breath. Addy could tell that Sam just loved it.

So Sam was there when Paul's next letter came. It said:

"My uncle died and I have to come to Indiana to help straighten things out. I'd like to come by to see Grendel. I had a lawyer look up her birth certificate, and I know she's mine. The way you were, I know you didn't have anyone else and, since you were pregnant when I left, she has to be my kid. I'll be there in about two weeks. Paul."

Addy sought Sam and blurted it all out. He listened. She ranted and raged, and he let it run its course. She said, "This is 'worse.'" When he looked blank, she elaborated, "'For better or for worse'? This is a worse."

"It isn't even close to worse," Sam reassured her. "You have no problem whatsoever. He can't take Grendel away from you. She's mine too. We wouldn't allow that. But, Addy, you can share her with her father."

What? Addy couldn't believe he'd want Grendel to even meet a man who had run from the responsibility of her, and she raged at him.

He lay back on the sofa, his hands behind his head, his face sympathetic and serious as he listened. Then he asked quietly, "Why do you feel so angry?"

She stopped, and her bosom heaved with emotion. Then she said, "I was so afraid. How could I know how it would be for a child? Would the child hate me? Be ashamed?"

Sam got up and went to her. He put his arms around her, and she clung to him. "Would you like a little swallow of brandy?"

"I need to think. I need a clear head."

"How about two vitamin C's?" he suggested. "They're good for stress."

"I need to walk."

They walked for quite a while. After they returned to the house, Addy continued to talk, to give vent to her feelings. She asked, "Why should Paul be allowed to share a child after he abandoned me and never even got in touch with me? Why should he have that privilege?"

"She's his child," Sam reminded her gently.

"Sure. All he contributed was one selfish sperm...and he claims she's his."

"She's a delight. She's a darling. He should know her."

"Yes. He's seen a picture of her and knows she's normal. What if Grendel had been an afflicted child?

What if her mind and body had been twisted? Would he be beating on the door demanding his 'right' to see her? Tracing her down and claiming her?" She turned on Sam and demanded, "Where was *he* these last four years?"

"Remember the woman at the museum who said, 'At least she'll know her father and be friends.' Don't you see that Grendel has rights too? She'd always be curious. This way she'll know him and, through him, the other half of her family."

"How do I know they won't snub her? How do I know he won't try to change her, give her all kinds of repressions and fears? He couldn't face my being pregnant. He couldn't face any responsibility. How can I know how he might influence her?"

"You could lock her up, make sure she doesn't see anyone." Then in the kindest possible way he took her shoulders in his hands and made her look at him as he said, "Addy, if you'll share Grendel with me, why not with her father?"

"You're *too* understanding!"

"No. I only think how it would be if I'd been Paul."

Without hesitation, she stated, "You would never have left me."

"No," he agreed, watching her. "Open your heart, Addy, and give this opportunity to Grendel."

"But Paul benefits."

"Is he such a monster?"

"Yes!" She was positive. Then she hesitated. Then she admitted, "No, not really. Let me think."

"Do unto others . . ." He slid that in very gently.

"That's what Miss Pru said after the first letter."

"He wrote before? You'd heard from him? How many times?"

"Just once. It was . . . oh . . . in March? I filed it away and forgot it."

"Did you?" Sam chided.

"No, I didn't really forget it, I tried to ignore it. He'd seen her picture in the *Journal* out in California and wrote and asked if she was his."

"Logical."

"Sam, I don't want him to see Grendel."

"Revenge?"

She admitted it. "Yes."

"You have two weeks to change your mind."

"I won't."

Ever afterward Addy recalled May's fall show as a fragmented, troubled dream. She lived through it vaguely aware of what was going on outside of herself. She knew it was a success. The word most used was "brilliant." Emmaline's scarves were snatched up almost shockingly. Two of the ladies even fought over one through clenched teeth! Addy's clients began to bring along friends to fittings so they could catch glimpses of the designs. Miss Pru said that had to stop, it led to too much confusion, but how could they stop the casual drop-ins without discouraging the business it brought?

Addy was no help. She argued with herself and at the silent Sam during the entire time before Paul's arrival. She went over and over the reasons to shun Paul, and she exhausted herself. Sam listened gravely and said little during those ten days. Then he did say, "I'm Grendel's father. Paul, being her sire, can't change that. But Paul deserves to see Grendel, and Grendel deserves to meet Paul. Even more important, you need to exorcise the bitterness you're nurturing."

"I have a right to be bitter!" she stormed.

"Yes. You did. But that's past. Don't let it eat away at you. I want all of you, and if you're harboring a lump of bitterness at another man, I'll be cheated."

"I wouldn't cheat you," she protested.

"You are now," Sam told her. "Most of your mind is taken up with this. We've only been married three weeks, but all I've heard from you is talk about another man." That startled her, so he added, "I thought I'd come first in your thinking."

"What have I been doing?" she exclaimed.

"Who's important? Paul?"

"You are!" She flung herself at him.

"And so is Grendel," he told her. Then he said again, "Allow Paul to meet her."

She leaned back in his arms to look into his face. "Do you really think I should?"

Sam didn't laugh or exclaim in exasperation; he only nodded seriously.

"All right," she said slowly. "I'll do it."

"That's great, Addy. You'll never regret it."

Paul phoned the next day. He'd counted the two weeks as including the time the letter took to get to Addy. They arranged that he would see Grendel the next day. Addy told Sam she wouldn't meet with Paul. He said she didn't have to this time, that he would.

"You be sure he doesn't kidnap her," Addy warned. "That happens . . ."

"Don't worry," Sam reassured her. "I'll be there."

"And as soon as the hour is up, run him out."

"Addy . . ."

"Well!" she retorted defensively.

"Quit worrying." He hugged her and commended, "You're being very good about this."

"No, I'm not. You're being very good about this, and I want you to think well of me."

"Whatever the reason, you're doing the right thing."

"Are you sure?" she asked worriedly.

"Umm-hmm."

"And you'll watch him every minute?"

"Addy . . ."

The next day, with her nerves twanging, Addy dressed Grendel nervously and looked at her critically—and she became very anxious. Grendel looked so darling, Paul was sure to snatch her up and run away with her. Addy frowned at a watching Sam, who shook his head slowly and smiled at her. "She looks so darling . . ." Addy began.

"Don't worry." Sam took a chattering Grendel downstairs to wait.

Addy stayed in their room upstairs, waiting. She couldn't sit still and fidgeted and paced and finally went to the front windows and peered out through the lace curtains. What would Paul look like? She had a vague memory of him as a reflection of Grendel, but since she had no picture of him, she couldn't actually remember.

He was on time. She watched him get out of a car and look up at the house and lick his lips. He was nervous. He straightened his cuffs and pulled his jacket down needlessly and fingered his tie. Then he took a deep breath and let it all out and walked purposefully up toward the porch.

It was an ordeal for him! He was scared and nervous. How strange. And he was smaller than she remembered. She'd forgotten how his beard shadowed his face blue, even as cleanly shaven as he was. She crept to the top of the stairs and squatted down behind the banister to watch from that hidden vantage point as the doorbell pealed.

Sam came into the entrance hall below and opened the front door. He introduced himself easily, and Paul exclaimed he hadn't realized Addy was married . . . the

Kildaire . . . Sam replied they'd just been married on the fifteenth. Paul shook Sam's hand nervously and congratulated him awkwardly as his eyes took in the lovely entrance hall and the grand staircase. His eyes didn't reach up to Addy's hidden site.

Then Grendel came into the hall, walking on tiptoe like a curious fairy in the woods. Her hands were up, her little neck stretched, her movements lyrical.

Paul's face suffused with color and he gasped softly, "My God," as he saw his child.

Sam turned and held out his hand as he said, "Grendel, here is someone who has come to meet you."

She smiled and walked over to Sam and took his hand as she looked up at the stranger.

"This is your father," Sam explained.

Grendel laughed. "No, silly, you are!" And with both of her hands in Sam's she swung there, off balance, playing.

Paul sank to his knees, his eyes glued to the child, and again he whispered hoarsely, "My God."

Sam was saying to Grendel, "Yes, I know. I'm your daddy, but he's your father. His name is Paul Morris."

"How do you do?" Grendel spaced out the words and swung one foot as she leaned against Sam's leg and held on to his hand.

Paul held out his hand, his face red and his eyes watery as he asked Grendel, "May I hold your hand?" His voice was unsteady.

Grendel looked all the way up to Sam's face to see if she should, and Sam nodded. Not letting go of Sam, Grendel gave her other hand to Paul, but she didn't move close to him. Her tiny hand lay in his and again he said, "My God," and his voice cracked.

"Are you crying?" Grendel asked with interest.

"Let's go into the parlor," Sam suggested kindly. And

he moved so that Paul could rise to his feet easily. Then Sam said to Grendel, "Tell him who Stormy is, Grendel."

They moved out of Addy's sight into the parlor, and she found tears on her cheeks. Still on her knees, she heard a soft sniff and turned to find Miss Pru discreetly blowing her nose. They looked at each other with all the knowledge of their times together, and Miss Pru touched Addy's head in a gentle way before she turned to go back to her room.

Filled with a strange, unknown emotion, Addy sat down, cross-legged. At a sound, she turned and saw that Sam was coming up the stairs to her. She could hear the murmur of Paul's voice, punctuated by Grendel's high-pitched, little-girl's voice coming from the parlor.

Reaching the top of the stairs, Sam stood there and smiled down at Addy before he put out his hand to help her rise to her feet. A little self-conscious, she wiped her wet cheeks and felt awkward. Would he think the tears were from seeing Paul again?

"Will you come down?" Sam whispered.

She shook her head. "Not this time." And with those words, she knew she was healed. She'd acknowledged the fact that Paul would visit Grendel again, and that she could see him. "I don't know why I'm crying."

"When you share something beautiful with another person, it touches your heart."

She looked up at Sam and saw tears in his own eyes. She knew then that he understood it all. She was at last free of her obsession, and she saw that he was proud of her. "Oh, Sam," she said. "I love you."

WATCH FOR
6 NEW TITLES EVERY MONTH!

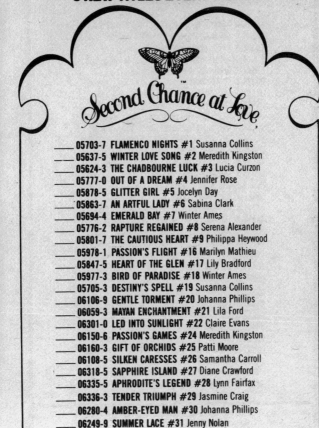

Second Chance at Love

____ 06424-6 **GARDEN OF SILVERY DELIGHTS** #42 Sharon Francis
____ 06521-8 **STRANGE POSSESSION** #43 Johanna Phillips
____ 06326-6 **CRESCENDO** #44 Melinda Harris
____ 05818-1 **INTRIGUING LADY** #45 Daphne Woodward
____ 06547-1 **RUNAWAY LOVE** #46 Jasmine Craig
____ 06423-8 **BITTERSWEET REVENGE** #47 Kelly Adams
____ 06541-2 **STARBURST** #48 Tess Ewing
____ 06540-4 **FROM THE TORRID PAST** #49 Ann Cristy
____ 06544-7 **RECKLESS LONGING** #50 Daisy Logan
____ 05851-3 **LOVE'S MASQUERADE** #51 Lillian Marsh
____ 06148-4 **THE STEELE HEART** #52 Jocelyn Day
____ 06422-X **UNTAMED DESIRE** #53 Beth Brookes
____ 06651-6 **VENUS RISING** #54 Michelle Roland
____ 06595-1 **SWEET VICTORY** #55 Jena Hunt
____ 06575-7 **TOO NEAR THE SUN** #56 Aimee Duvall
____ 05625-1 **MOURNING BRIDE** #57 Lucia Curzon
____ 06411-4 **THE GOLDEN TOUCH** #58 Robin James
____ 06596-X **EMBRACED BY DESTINY** #59 Simone Hadary
____ 06660-5 **TORN ASUNDER** #60 Ann Cristy
____ 06573-0 **MIRAGE** #61 Margie Michaels
____ 06650-8 **ON WINGS OF MAGIC** #62 Susanna Collins
____ 05816-5 **DOUBLE DECEPTION** #63 Amanda Troy
____ 06675-3 **APOLLO'S DREAM** #64 Claire Evans
____ 06680-X **THE ROGUE'S LADY** #69 Anne Devon
____ 06687-7 **FORSAKING ALL OTHERS** #76 LaVyrle Spencer
____ 06689-3 **SWEETER THAN WINE** #78 Jena Hunt
____ 06690-7 **SAVAGE EDEN** #79 Diane Crawford
____ 06691-5 **STORMY REUNION** #80 Jasmine Craig
____ 06692-3 **THE WAYWARD WIDOW** #81 Anne Mayfield
____ 06693-1 **TARNISHED RAINBOW** #82 Jocelyn Day
____ 06694-X **STARLIT SEDUCTION** #83 Anne Reed
____ 06695-8 **LOVER IN BLUE** #84 Aimee Duvall

All of the above titles are $175 per copy

Available at your local bookstore or return this form to:

SECOND CHANCE AT LOVE
Book Mailing Service
P.O. Box 690, Rockville Centre, NY 11571

Please send me the titles checked above. I enclose _____
Include $1.00 for postage and handling if one book is ordered; 50¢ per book for
two or more. California, Illinois, New York and Tennessee residents please add
sales tax.

NAME _____

ADDRESS _____

CITY _____ STATE/ZIP _____
(allow six weeks for delivery)   SK-41

_____ 06696-6 THE FAMILIAR TOUCH #85 Lynn Lawrence
_____ 06697-4 TWILIGHT EMBRACE #86 Jennifer Rose
_____ 06698-2 QUEEN OF HEARTS #87 Lucia Curzon
_____ 06850-0 PASSION'S SONG #88 Johanna Phillips
_____ 06851-9 A MAN'S PERSUASION #89 Katherine Granger
_____ 06852-7 FORBIDDEN RAPTURE #90 Kate Nevins
_____ 06853-5 THIS WILD HEART #91 Margarett McKean
_____ 06854-3 SPLENDID SAVAGE #92 Zandra Colt
_____ 06855-1 THE EARL'S FANCY #93 Charlotte Hines
_____ 06858-6 BREATHLESS DAWN #94 Susanna Collins
_____ 06859-4 SWEET SURRENDER #95 Diana Mars
_____ 06860-8 GUARDED MOMENTS #96 Lynn Fairfax
_____ 06861-6 ECSTASY RECLAIMED #97 Brandy LaRue
_____ 06862-4 THE WIND'S EMBRACE #98 Melinda Harris
_____ 06863-2 THE FORGOTTEN BRIDE #99 Lillian Marsh
_____ 06864-0 A PROMISE TO CHERISH #100 LaVyrle Spencer
_____ 06865-9 GENTLE AWAKENING #101 Marianne Cole
_____ 06866-7 BELOVED STRANGER #102 Michelle Roland
_____ 06867-5 ENTHRALLED #103 Ann Cristy
_____ 06868-3 TRIAL BY FIRE #104 Faye Morgan
_____ 06869-1 DEFIANT MISTRESS #105 Anne Devon
_____ 06870-5 RELENTLESS DESIRE #106 Sandra Brown
_____ 06871-3 SCENES FROM THE HEART #107 Marie Charles
_____ 06872-1 SPRING FEVER #108 Simone Hadary
_____ 06873-X IN THE ARMS OF A STRANGER #109 Deborah Joyce
_____ 06874-8 TAKEN BY STORM #110 Kay Robbins
_____ 06899-3 THE ARDENT PROTECTOR #111 Amanda Kent
_____ 07200-1 A LASTING TREASURE #112 Cally Hughes $1.95
_____ 07201-X RESTLESS TIDES #113 Kelly Adams $1.95
_____ 07202-8 MOONLIGHT PERSUASION #114 Sharon Stone $1.95
_____ 07203-6 COME WINTER'S END #115 Claire Evans $1.95
_____ 07204-4 LET PASSION SOAR #116 Sherry Carr $1.95
_____ 07205-2 LONDON FROLIC #117 (Regency) Josephine Janes $1.95

All of the above titles are $1.75 per copy except where noted

Available at your local bookstore or return this form to:

SECOND CHANCE AT LOVE
Book Mailing Service
P.O. Box 690, Rockville Centre, NY 11571

Please send me the titles checked above. I enclose _____
Include $1.00 for postage and handling if one book is ordered; 50¢ per book for
two or more. California, Illinois, New York and Tennessee residents please add
sales tax.

NAME _____

ADDRESS _____

CITY _____ STATE/ZIP _____

(allow six weeks for delivery)   SK-41

WHAT READERS SAY ABOUT
SECOND CHANCE AT LOVE BOOKS

"Your books are the greatest!"
—*M. N., Carteret, New Jersey**

"I have been reading romance novels for quite some time, but the SECOND CHANCE AT LOVE books are the most enjoyable."
—*P. R., Vicksburg, Mississippi**

"I enjoy SECOND CHANCE [AT LOVE] more than any books that I have read and I do read a lot."
—*J. R., Gretna, Louisiana**

"I really think your books are exceptional . . . I read Harlequin and Silhouette and although I still like them, I'll buy your books over theirs. SECOND CHANCE [AT LOVE] is more interesting and holds your attention and imagination with a better story line . . ."
—*J. W., Flagstaff, Arizona**

"I've read many romances, but yours take the 'cake'!"
—*D. H., Bloomsburg, Pennsylvania**

"Have waited ten years for *good* romance books. Now I have them."
—*M. P., Jacksonville, Florida**

*Names and addresses available upon request